Books by Geoffrey Household

Novels

The Third Hour
Rogue Male
Arabesque
The High Place
A Rough Shoot
A Time to Kill
Fellow Passenger

Watcher in the Shadows
Thing to Love
Olura
The Courtesy of Death
Dance of the Dwarfs
Doom's Caravan
The Three Sentinels

The Lives and Times of Bernardo Brown
Red Anger
Hostage: London

Autobiography

Against the Wind

Short Stories

The Salvation of Pisco Gabar
Tale of Adventurers
The Brides of Solomon and Other Stories
Sabres on the Sand

For Children

The Exploits of Xenophon
The Spanish Cave
Prisoner of the Indies
Escape into Daylight

HOSTAGE
London

HOSTAGE
London

The Diary of Julian Despard

Geoffrey Household

An Atlantic Monthly Press Book

Little, Brown and Company
Boston   Toronto

FIRST AMERICAN EDITION

T 04/77

Library of Congress Cataloging in Publication Data

Household, Geoffrey, 1900–
  Hostage—London.

  "An Atlantic Monthly Press book."
  I. Title.
PZ3.A8159Ho3   [PR6015.07885]   823'.9'12   76-53841
ISBN 0-316-37437-7

ATLANTIC–LITTLE, BROWN BOOKS
ARE PUBLISHED BY
LITTLE, BROWN AND COMPANY
IN ASSOCIATION WITH
THE ATLANTIC MONTHLY PRESS

Designed by Christine Benders

Published simultaneously in Canada
by Little, Brown & Company (Canada) Limited

PRINTED IN THE UNITED STATES OF AMERICA

HOSTAGE
London

June 2nd

I have never been so moved by the beauty of our earth. Excitement of course sharpens the senses. Man is still enough of an animal to be far more keenly observant when he is in danger or engaged in illegalities; but I know that at any time I should have responded to the stillness and colors of the inlet and the strangely decisive shape of the cliff which faced me across the water.

I lay among the terraces of olive on the steep northern slope of the cove with nothing to do till after sundown, and probably nothing then. In an emergency I could reach the edge of the water by following a precipitous goat track which cut down through the crumbling stone walls. My orders were to delay or distract any interference on this, the only accessible side. It was unlikely that there would be any, for the water was out of sight of the scattered village behind and above me and two cottages at the head of the inlet were safely tucked away up a winding valley. It may be that some money had passed to ensure that the fishermen and their families stayed indoors or visited the cinema. At any rate, I was told that I need not worry about them.

The sheer face of yellowish rock opposite me started at a height of perhaps two hundred feet and slanted downwards across the south side of the cove until it turned the corner and plunged into the open sea. The crest was a straight diagonal line separated from the sky by a narrow band of olive; at its foot was the brilliance of blue water sparkling in the evening sun. It may have been the diagonal which created the multiformity of beauty, as if

3

one were to paint a three-sided landscape, the bottom horizontal, the frame then running up from the lower right-hand corner at an angle of thirty degrees. It was an uncompromising frame, and its regularity, enhancing the richness and detail of living earth by a sort of cosmic horizon, was at a guess what moved me to rejoice in the unknowable purpose it served. I haven't anything which could fairly be called religion beyond a vague reluctance to ascribe too much to accident.

In the short dusk I moved lower down the slope so that I would be within reach of the boat when it arrived. There I commanded the path to the water and an even rougher one which followed the lowest tiers of olive to the head of the cove. The only sounds were from the distant village: a final cockcrow and the bleating of goats. There was no wind. Even if a norther had suddenly sprung up, the cove was sheltered. That small indentation in the savage northwest coast of Paxos had been well chosen. I was told that shipping rarely came close in, apart from tourist caïques doing the round of the island in fine weather and the occasional boat of a lobster fisherman.

An hour before the moon rose the motor cruiser was lying under the cliff. She had cut her engines and put out the lights, and I would not have known she was there if not for the muffled sounds of wood on wood and wood on metal as her cargo was manhandled for easier trans-shipment. The coaster was bang on time a quarter of an hour later. The black bulk of her, darker than the night, could be distinguished and the throb of the diesels heard, but there was no risk that she would be identified since

4

the operation was carried out too swiftly for anyone to stumble down through the olive groves and interrupt it. In any case, I doubt if police or coast guards kept an eye on the northwestern cliffs, where approachable beaches were few and small, and only two could be reached from inland.

I heard the coaster's derrick swing out and lift a load from the cruiser. In five minutes more both craft had left the cove. When the coaster was a few miles out, with no other shipping in sight, she put on her lights and would have seemed to any observer to be on course from Preveza to Brindisi. I saw no more of the cruiser.

For a while I stayed on in the silver peace and silence after the moon had risen — partly because I felt I ought to make certain that no one else showed any interest in the cove, and partly because I was reluctant to leave that little secluded meadow of the sea, the memory of which will haunt me for ever. A mixture of motives so curious that one must probably be untrue. I cannot say which.

Following my orders, I returned to my sleeping bag on the other side of the island without meeting a soul. Early in the morning I took the daily packet to Corfu with my bedroll on my back, inconspicuous among other holiday-makers. It was a rough passage against a norther, and I wondered whether the cruiser had put in for shelter and where. In the evening I was back in London, apparently after a weekend in the sun.

My knowledge of the reasons for the operation is very limited. I know the motor cruiser came from Libya, taking some thirty-six hours. I can guess that the cargo transshipped was a crate of arms or explosives, but whether for us or for Ulster or Italy is not my business as a cell leader. I am trained to obey, to ask no questions, and to care for the safety of my partisans.

June 10th

That last entry was originally just a casual, personal note, an undated aid to recollection. Now that I have decided to keep a record of events I have put a date on it. The night of June 2nd is where this diary should start.

Why a diary? Because I am uneasy; because I cannot make sense of the operation, and weekly or daily details of which I do not yet see the importance may take on a definite meaning when I refer to them later. Such a diary is, I admit, a menace to the security of Magma, but I am confident it will never be read. I have treated every tenth page and inserted into the padded cover of a luxurious yearbook — designed with conspicuous vulgarity for the desk of some producer of superfluous rubbish — a small incendiary device which will infallibly destroy it if opened by anyone but myself.

Four days after my return to London, the press carried a story of the hijacking of a consignment of arms from a beach in Libya on the night of May 31st. Surprisingly, responsible papers, as well as the more sensational rags, made it front-page news, giving a small theft as much publicity as if we had robbed the Bank of France. France I mention because the security conferences which so excite the media seem to be taking place in Paris. Interpol has been called in. The papers always report this to impress us with the enormity of the crime, though Interpol is hardly more than a center of hot lines connecting one set of peaked caps with another.

After allowing for speculative additions and the usual omission of solid facts, here is the approximate picture:

A motor cruiser, the *Chaharazad*, was discreetly taking delivery of the arms on a deserted beach not far from Benghazi — as likely as not, all that remained of a long vanished port. When she arrived a truck was already waiting. The Lebanese owner and his deckhand went ashore, approaching the truck without any special caution, and were quickly nobbled by three masked men. The hijackers then went aboard the cruiser, held up the master and engineer, and locked all four in the small forward cabin.

The prisoners heard the crate being loaded and the engines starting up just before dawn. For a day, a night, and most of the next day the *Chaharazad* proceeded at her cruising speed of about fourteen knots — so far as they could tell — and in the evening began to idle along. They were then blindfolded and tied up. The master, apparently a temperamental and indignant Greek, dared to resist; he was immediately shot dead and thrown overboard. After that the remaining three gave no trouble at all.

Soon after dark they heard the cargo transshipped to some other vessel. A few hours later, still tied up and blindfolded, they were set ashore in the cruiser's dinghy, and it was not until late next day that they were spotted by fishermen on a remote and inaccessible pebble bank below the western cliffs of the tiny island of Antipaxos.

At first these three surviving Lebanese stated merely that the *Chaharazad* had been hijacked and that at least one of the hijackers was British. They didn't say a word about arms until that side of the story was publicized by the Libyan Government. Now, since the Libyans are known to be supplying arms to the Palestinians, to Ulster, and to any revolutionary organization which has the money, why on earth set the cat among the pigeons by admitting what the cruiser was up to and inviting investigation? They could have allowed the Lebanese story to stand.

I have no doubt that this was the transshipment I witnessed and that Magma is responsible. We can be proud of an operation brilliantly plotted and carried out on the strength of first-class inside information. The death of the master is regrettable but could not be helped. Yet I would dearly like to know what sense there can be in so much planning and expense to acquire a crate of arms. As yet we do not need more than the small quantity available for emergencies, and there is no shortage of explosives.

So my curiosity is natural, but again I ask myself: why a diary? Even assuming that the story carried by all the media is true — and it tallies closely with the little I know of the truth — I am in no danger. I obeyed orders and have no reason to question them.

Do I then have reason to question myself? That may be the answer. Accident has thrown me between two mysteries. If I had supervised this transshipment in, say, the London docks, I should have downed a few triumphant drinks with my partisans and thought no more of it. If I had been a casual traveler in Paxos, I should never have forgotten sea and cliff and the silent passing of color into night, but dissociated it completely from my life of revolutionary violence. It could be the combination of the two which provokes a need for confession, separating myself into both sinner and priest.

The obscenities of the society I seek to destroy are definite, while the beauty which I may destroy with them is unknown and unlimited. A statement of the obvious. Preserve the blossom and your insecticide destroys the bees. Control the flooding and you pollute the estuary. We can never foresee the appalling damage done by long-range good intentions and I suspect that the Cosmic Purpose cannot foresee it either, that it is in fact a Cosmic Experimenter.

Well, here is the successor to the dinosaurs — a running ape which can question its motives and use paw and pencil to resolve them. I will assume for the moment that all I wish to record for future reference is the marked element of risk in this operation which seems unwise and out of character.

The daylight voyage of June 1st was safe enough, assuming there were no witnesses to the hijacking, but the day of June 2nd must have been anxious if the real arms dealers turned up on the beach shortly after the *Chaharazad* had sailed and found an inexplicably empty truck. I suppose we counted on delay in discovering what had actually happened and the time it takes to search the emptiness of the sea.

According to the papers the cruiser has vanished, though she was bound to call somewhere to refuel. Obviously the hijackers sank her the same night after landing their prisoners, themselves going secretly ashore in the dinghy and sinking that too — not difficult if they opened the bilge cock, lashed the tiller, and gave her a push with the engine running.

From a police point of view the coaster is the weakest link in the chain. It's not all that hard to find a captain with a carefully selected crew who will take on clandestine cargo so long as he is convinced that foolproof arrangements have been made for smuggling it into its destination; but the convincing is easier than the organization on shore. I hope we expected all this excitement and are one imaginative jump ahead of port security officers. Fortunately the blindfolded Lebanese can give no information about the size of the ship.

The destination cannot be Italy or farther along the coast of North Africa, for the *Chaharazad* could reach either as easily as Paxos. Then Spain, France or Germany? In all three countries the national committees would have undertaken the job themselves, claiming to be more experienced. So England seems the most likely. All merchant shipping sailing from the eastern Mediterranean at the right time will be under suspicion, with the closest watch on the coast of Northern Ireland. In fact, Magma has only a very limited interest in those religious fanatics.

Clotilde visits me tomorrow, but there is little hope of getting any hint from her. She sometimes carries security too far, not realizing that it is unwise for a group commander to arouse too much curiosity in the cell leaders. I think that as a woman she feels she should show herself a more severe disciplinarian than any man. But God knows I've no complaint of her efficiency! When she sent me to Paxos her orders were detailed and precise. I knew exactly what I was to do and nothing of why I was doing it. A fault on the right side. I couldn't even have invented a reasonable story under torture.

Her procedures are never unnecessarily complicated. Because she visits me openly, the cell believes she is my girlfriend; I am sure none of them suspect that she is in fact the group commander. In their eyes she is a natural and romantic mate for their leader — a tall, handsome creature who would manage to look desirable even in uniform. Actually I find her too overpowering. I would not have been tempted even before my prison sentence. Since then I have been celibate as a priest, merciless to myself, compassionate towards all believers.

June 12th

Clotilde instructed me to call a meeting of my cell and explain to them a change of policy. There would be no more attempts to release prisoners by the taking of hostages or other threats.

It has always seemed to me that there is a logical flaw in the taking of hostages. Kill your hostage and that's the end of you by gunfire or life imprisonment. Don't kill your hostage, and what the hell is the good of him?

There is also the difficulty of finding any sure home for a rescued partisan. We have been too successful. The Communists now are as frightened of us as the rest, all vaguely suspecting a unity behind the diversity of terrorists. Undoubtedly we are about to reach a deadlock, where no state will accept prisoners released by blackmail and no aircraft carrying such passengers will be allowed to land.

Given a threat sufficiently impressive, it might be possible to insist that the prisoner should live freely wherever he or she wished without leaving the country. I asked Clotilde if she thought that point worth discussion.

"Live as a pariah? Avoided by the public and watched by the police?"

"We could do what was done for me — change of appearance and identity."

"It was new and difficult. You were a specially important case. The ideal solution is to become so powerful that we never have to release prisoners because none are arrested."

"We are bound to lose some."

She made no comment, would not be drawn out, and refused to argue. I avoided any awkwardness by asking whether the shipment had arrived safely.

She looked through me, still on her guard, as if my question had not been a mere change of subject but had some connection with this business of avoiding arrest.

"Not yet," she replied. "Your cell should be ready for orders at any time."

The fundamental rule is to limit the knowledge of any operation to a single cell whenever possible; so I had expected we might be engaged in the landing of the crate and was glad to hear that we should be. I admit that action is a drug. All the same I enjoy it. I must have been wholly misplaced as a lecturer in sociology, always a little bored by my own influence. If ten years ago I had accepted without question the obscenities of capitalist mass democracy instead of loathing them, I might now be a young major in the army. What a devastating thought!

Clotilde often accuses me of being battle-happy. She herself is as detached as any general sending hundreds to death; but the general wouldn't have much success unless a satisfying number of them were battle-happy. However, her reading of me may be right. It is to be expected after guerrilla courses in Jordan and North Korea — which really taught me no more than basic tactics — and the more valuable short spell in Uruguay to learn how those tactics could be applied to urban conditions.

"Before Paxos I did not know that we were strong at sea," I said.

There must have been a competent navigator. It looks easy enough to hit Paxos by sailing due north from Benghazi, but allowances must be made for wind and currents. An amateur yachtsman, staying safely out from the islands, would very likely miss Paxos altogether.

"We are strong in Glasgow, Liverpool and Hamburg."

All of them hotbeds of communism. I asked her if they had had much success in infiltrating our cells.

"Not since two were found drowned," she replied.

It is not very difficult to spot a Communist. He or she has it all pat but is inclined to pretend enthusiasm for urban guerrilla activity in Russia and Eastern Europe. The time for that will come when their police states show signs of breaking down under their own weight. Only then can Magma launch the New Revolution and see that the mad economy of the West does not take the place of state capitalism.

Clotilde left soon afterwards. I would have liked to ask her what on earth the Libyans thought they were up to with all that unnecessary publicity, but I may already have given the impression of wanting to know too much. I hope to God I shall be told enough if my cell is to be responsible for landing or concealing the arms. The ingenuity of the Action Committee and their exact working out of every detail command my fascinated admiration although they do occasionally overlook the human element, cheerfully assuming that a devoted partisan is superhuman. And sometimes he is. Well, it's my job as a leader, I suppose, to lay out the pieces for the chess masters and see that the legs under the table do not give way.

June 15th

A successful operation, though I am appalled by the expense of it. I know that we are in funds and I suspect that we, not the Ulster Defense Association, pulled off the Midland Bank job in Dublin; but how the Action Committee works out what is value for money and what is not defeats me.

I was told that the freighter — a rather larger ship than my fleeting impression of her — was bound for Cardiff with currants and wine and that she carried the crate as deck cargo. On the night when she entered the Bristol Channel it would be lifted off her directly and quickly by helicopter and carried to the waiting lorry.

Clotilde ordered me to take one of my partisans and drive an open truck to a lane near Kentisbury on the high grassland of Exmoor, arriving at 11:15 P.M. Two hooded

14

landing lights were to be turned on and off as soon as the sound of the helicopter was heard. The load would be slung beneath it and lowered directly on to the transport. We had only to unhook the cable. It was considered most unlikely that there would be any traffic in the lane during the few minutes of the operation, but we should be supplied with Devon County Council notices of ROAD CLOSED to be planted at both ends. When the crate was on board we were to drive to Blackmoor Gate, where the truck would be taken over by another team. A third member of my cell with a car would be stationed near the crossroads so that my party could be driven home.

It was a journey of about two hundred miles from London, so I started early in the afternoon in case of delay. It was as well that I did, for the gas line gave trouble. Fortunately I had with me Mick, who is a competent mechanic. He had been an International Marxist in the Northeast, specializing in industrial sabotage. He once told me that he had been bored by the futility of it, that our industrial workers were as mischievous as a band of monkeys. All they wanted was to thumb a collective nose at management. They had never given a thought to the New Revolution — beyond cheering any mention of any revolution — and they supported Labour as enthusiastically as their football team; its job was to win. The idealist in Mick was disillusioned — unreasonably, I think. The picture he drew was that of a healthy, hearty, sly and cynical society waiting to be presented with an ideal worth working for.

We reached Blackmoor Gate at ten and I checked that the car for our return was waiting there, driven by my ever-reliable Elise. She had backed off the road, and it would have taken us some time to find her if she had not walked out to meet us; she and the car were invisible, well hidden behind a bank. A typical urban guerrilla. She could place a bomb with absolute coolness and courage, but to be alone on wild, high ground with no other companions than the soft wind from the Atlantic and the rustlings and silences of the grass was a bit much for her. I told her to drive down to Ilfracombe, have some coffee and a sandwich, and be back by 11:15.

We, too, had to keep driving, for it was unwise to park in a town or the middle of nowhere and invite questions from any passing police. Our truck was pink with brick dust and marked with the name of Groads Construction Company. Mick noticed that the door panel and side boards could be quickly removed and substituted, changing the name and address of the firm without the necessity of repainting. He thought five minutes in a dark street or on a municipal tip would be enough.

At zero hour we were in the lane with our lights out. Somebody at the top has an eye for country and, to judge by the perfect choices of this lonely upland and the Paxos cove, always does a personal reconnaissance. Open grass. High banks topped by straggling hawthorn on both sides of the lane. Not a light to be seen but the dim graying of the sky by a lighthouse beam, probably on faraway Lundy.

We had a disturbingly long wait and it was after 11:30 when we heard the helicopter coming in from the northwest. At once we put out the ROAD CLOSED signs and began to flash the landing lights. That was the only risk I disapproved of, but it was more apparent than real. If anyone did notice the narrow shafts against a dark background, we should be well away by the time he came up to investigate, leaving nothing behind us but a rumor to tantalize the interest of the Customs and the UFO fans.

The helicopter hovered over us, picked out the truck in its own floodlamp, and lowered the crate. It was smaller than I had expected and had French markings which described the contents as graphite. We cast off the cable, gathered up signs and landing lights, and in three minutes were off to Blackmoor Gate. The racket of the helicopter disappeared in the direction of the Welsh coast. I presume that there was no evidence that the pilot had ever left it. The flight across the water from, say, Swansea was about fifty miles, so that he had only to account for an hour of his time, which he could well do by faking engine trouble and coming down with no witness but mountain sheep.

At Blackmoor Gate a party of three were off the road with Elise. I knew none of them but two knew me, addressing me by my nom de guerre of Gil. Therefore they would not be partisans from another cell or group but members of the Action Committee. If I am any judge of faces, one of them was the unknown planner. He was a tiger of a man, with eyes that seemed to reflect light even when there wasn't any and a pointed beard. His oil-stained overalls could not disguise a loose, prowling body built for endurance rather than athletics. I was sure that he, too, had had paramilitary training and would be happily at home on hilltops or at sea.

He took over command without question and thoroughly checked the truck. He was not in the least rattled when two cars passed and asked if he needed help. Meanwhile I calmed down the third man of their party — a tall, weedy fellow with strands of hair blowing in the breeze. I thought that perhaps he came from some university as I had before the disaster and my sentence. He kept on telling me how essential it was to get away and babbled about packing as if the crate contained detonators. He evidently assumed that I knew what it did contain, and his indiscretion made it certain that he was not a member of any cell, was not trained in the discipline, and had never before been engaged in any active operation.

We drove away by different roads — they along the coast to Bridgwater and Bristol, my party to South Molton. I sat in the front with Elise and we allowed ourselves to admire or pretend to admire Clotilde. Elise quite rightly thinks she is the wrong woman for me but would not dream of saying so. A thousand years ago Clotilde would have made the perfect wife for a feudal baron and ridden to battle with him, the long, fair hair flowing from her helmet. I can imagine the pale, dark Elise staying at home and inspiring wistful songs from troubadours. A flame of a girl unselfishly prepared to be blown out — or up.

Her hatred of our society stems from her experience of physical starvation in the Third World rather than the spiritual starvation of our own. As a medical student in her fourth year, she joined a relief expedition to the southern edge of the Sahara. There was little relief they could give but to revive the almost dead for a few short weeks until they were truly dead and desiccated. She once told me how, when she returned, it was the advertisements, the costly, lying, snob advertisements of the affluent society, which convinced her that there was no possible building on such a culture until it was utterly destroyed.

Elise tried to pump me. She, too, while waiting for us had talked to the wispy-haired stranger and noticed that he fidgeted and chirped to himself. Her impression was that the crate contained something live. Biological warfare? But even allowing for the international strength of Magma, we are not ready for direct confrontation with the State till we have aroused in the public a burning sense of its futility, and resentment followed by violent hatred.

My instinct that it would be as well to keep a very private record of events turns out to be right. Libya, Paxos, Exmoor, this whole caper for the sake of nothing but detonators or infected fleas to be planted on politicians — if anyone can tell the difference — simply does not make sense.

June 29th

Clotilde and two partisans have been arrested. My own cell was not engaged, so I know nothing about their attack on the Telephone Exchange. It looks as if the reconnaissance of the exchange was careless or else Special Branch has cleverly made security guards so inconspicuous that even Post Office supervisors do not know who they are. The urban guerrilla has still a lot to learn from freedom fighters in open country.

It was an ambitious job, which would have interrupted communications all over the Southeast, and evidently was considered too big for a cell leader to direct alone. But what a risk to involve Clotilde! However, if it had to be taken there could be no better choice. She'll refuse to talk and tell them to go to hell. The papers give me her real name, which of course I never knew: Alexandra Baratov; secretary; British mother, Russian father. The Russian father is useful, implying Communist or Trotskyist intrigue.

The three of them will have thrown suspicion on the extreme left without a mention of Magma, probably claiming to be members of the Workers Revolutionary Party. I suspect that Special Branch knows next to nothing of our existence, though they must be puzzled by an organizing ability and a command of funds far beyond those of such incompetents as the International Marxists.

A long sentence is inevitable, for they were caught red-handed when concealing the charges. The only comfort is that we will get her out eventually. If escape and change of identity could be arranged for me, it can be for her. The taking of hostages for her release is out, now that no country, even Algeria, will receive rescued prisoners.

July 4th

I have been appointed group commander in Clotilde's place and am responsible for eight cells. I am surprised to find that in London there are only three, the others being in the Midlands, with the primary objective of disrupting

20

production lines. Security at cell level turns out to be as faultless as I had thought. My cell leaders know only that the cover name of their group commander is Gil and how he will identify himself. All communication is person to person. I visit the cell leaders as Clotilde used to visit me. No addresses. No telephone numbers. The result is that a partisan in the hands of the police is unable to give anything away but the names of his cell members and its leader. The leader can only reveal the nom de guerre of his group commander — which is no more use than saying he occasionally descends from heaven.

As a critic of society I must confess a tendency to criticize. Speed of communication is sacrificed for the sake of security; as cell leader I could not contact Clotilde. When the time comes for us to challenge and disrupt the State instead of simply making well-timed stabs in the back, I believe we could adopt for the cells, without much loss of security, the link between group commander and Action Committee. I know by sight the four members of the committee who interviewed and approved me. I know where the meeting took place but not where the next one will be. I do not know where the international headquarters are. I do not know the true name of Rex, who is to give me my orders, but I can in an emergency get in touch with him. That loose-limbed tiger of a man whom I saw at Blackmoor Gate was at the meeting. "Bearded like the pard" comes to mind. I suspect that he is our delegate to the International Committee.

I have appointed Mick to take over the cell, chiefly because I am fond of him. Blind obedience is not his forte, but so long as he resists the temptation to show too much independence he may do better on his own than under me. He came to the New Revolution by way of the National Students' Union, seeing them as the natural leaders of the proletariat — a mistake the French made — and found that in fact he could lead but not as a self-confessed student. The man is by nature an actor and quick to learn, so he studied two regional accents for his part. He can do you a fiery speech in almost unintelligible Newcastle or hideous Birmingham. Magma made use of him and took him on when sheer disillusion was beginning to affect his oratory. I have trained him in urban tactics, night movement and concealment so far as can be done with just the pair of us. Elise, so passionately militant, has not enough respect for him because he does not know one end of a detonator from the other — or didn't until I taught him. I remember explaining to her that Mick could do more long-lasting damage to the consumer society than a ton of gelignite.

July 11th

The police have withdrawn the case against Clotilde and her two partisans on the grounds of mistaken identity. I cannot understand it at all, for the evidence against them must have been overwhelming. The press does not know what to make of it either. Some of the papers attack the police for too precipitate action, as if a store detective had arrested an absentminded duchess for shoplifting. Two of the Establishment papers play the whole thing down — a paragraph in a back page. Editors must have been given a tactful hint of something the public is not allowed to know. We can't possibly have been able to blackmail the Home Office.

Perhaps the Government believes that the criminals belong to some bunch of right-wing rats all smeared with Fascist sewage who have crept out of a friendly bourgeois state to which we are heavily in debt. In that case the Home Office might hush it all up and the Foreign Office deal with the inexplicable lunacy through diplomatic channels.

July 13th

The regular rendezvous with Rex changes every week. This time it was an art gallery in Belgravia, where one may walk around with feigned interest and get into casual conversation with the man or woman who happens to be appreciating the same picture at the same moment.

Rex could pass as almost anything he pleased according to his style of dress. In the art gallery he might have just strolled by from one of the Belgravia embassies. When I first met him he looked informal enough for an off-duty football manager. He has a full, craggy face framed in an untidy mane and plays, I think, the daily game of a respectable left-wing Social Democrat. It wouldn't surprise me if next time he turns up as a convincing builder's foreman. But I may be romanticizing. The strength of Magma is that one is what one is and above suspicion.

We strolled into Green Park and sat down. I will try to reconstruct the conversation.

"Any questions, Gil?" he asked with a smile.

"Only if it's advisable for me to know the answers."

"It may be."

"Then how the hell did you get Clotilde off?"

"The Government found it too, well, embarrassing to hold her."

"She said something to me about partisans being free from arrest."

"Yes. For the moment they are. The committee wants to know how much you have guessed. You were in it nearly from the start, you see."

I replied that I hadn't any reasonable guess at all and was naturally curious. I hoped some day to know how the Blackmoor Gate operation had been planned and why. Then I asked him whether Clotilde was safe, for it was certain that every step of hers must have been followed by Special Branch after she left the court.

"Quite safe, but not in circulation. Outside the court was a crowd of reporters howling for her comments. One of them was a Magma partisan. A woman. Her paper had authorized her to offer ten thousand for Clotilde's exclusive story. She took Clotilde along to Fleet Street and into a private office. Clotilde went to the loo — very natural after all that excitement. It was the men's loo. That took very careful timing with all those sots rushing in and out for a pee. She came out as quite an imposing young man, hat on the back of her head and hair under it, and cleared off at the back of the building. Our girl raised hell very convincingly and was not suspected. I myself disliked having to risk her, for she's too valuable. The disappearance of Clotilde need not have been so hurried."

"You were there?"

24

"I sometimes have the run of the place."

No wonder our inside information is so good! Rex cannot of course be a well-known figure, but he might be a leader writer or columnist. He has a slight provincial accent, which suggests that he started on a local paper and made his way up to Fleet Street.

I waited for him to tell me the facts of Clotilde's inexplicable acquittal, but evidently he was not yet ready or authorized to put me in the whole picture. So I asked him what orders he had for me.

"A few draft manifestos. Imagine that the State is trying to claw itself out of the grave, and explain what must be done to push it back! All your old philosophy, Gil, and at the top of your form. Out of chaos will come Justice and Humanity. Keep it simple for the simple!"

"And no action?"

It was a long time since I had been limited to the intellectual side of the movement. I did not want to return to theory and a typewriter.

"We may have that for you too. Tomorrow. Same hour. At Watts's statue *Physical Energy* in Kensington Gardens. The committee's view of you is that you should know as much as Clotilde did."

July 14th

This morning I met him by Watts's rampaging horse. Too healthy and too openly powerful for a horse of the apocalypse. A concept of the last century. What would our own emblem be? An abstract unintelligible to the conservative masses. An abstract that might represent the

25

pressure of one continent upon another till the silent Magma surges up between the tectonic plates and the cities steam, ready for us to rebuild mercy and justice on the rubble.

There was a summer drizzle of warm rain, so we could not take chairs without drawing attention to two eccentrics. We walked briskly east, worthy citizens not to be done out of their daily exercise by the weather.

"Did you notice," he asked, "that the theft of arms in Libya was published at once to the foreign press, the embassies, Interpol — the lot?"

I replied that I did and could not understand it. In any case, nobody would put much trust in any Libyan statement.

"Without strong confirmation, no."

"Where did it come from? Magma?"

"Confirmation came direct from Paris."

I asked what Paris had to do with it.

"*La gloire,* Gil. Always *la gloire*. Military glory, commercial glory — without them we should find so many objectives out of reach. You are aware of the motives which induced the French to offer a nuclear reactor to Libya?"

Vaguely I was, I said, and it seemed to me a useful step on the way to nuclear warfare and chaos. But I could not see why the French should be so obliging.

Rex replied that it was a very simple bargain. Australia and New Zealand were raising so much hell about Pacific tests of nuclear weapons that the French wanted a new testing ground. They asked for a desert site in the empty south of Libya. The Libyans agreed, on condition that they be given a nuclear reactor.

"Why, Gil? Why do the Libyans with all that oil to provide electricity want a prestige luxury which they cannot possibly handle without foreign technicians? To score off Israel and possibly Egypt. Where there is nuclear power there is also the possibility of a weapon. And from the French point of view a reactor in Libya is a bait to attract still more contracts from the Third World which has no oil. Do you know anything about nuclear fission?"

"A lot less than any student of physics and a little more than general knowledge."

"That's about enough. The Libyans insisted that the fuel rods for their reactor should be manufactured in Libya, thus alarming their neighbors and reinforcing the bluff. The French didn't think much of that and had to refuse. Fuel rods are right at the limit of technical knowledge. You can't run them up in a shed with a team of half-educated colonels from the Ministry of Science, even allowing for all the enthusiasm of awakening Islam.

"So then it was the Libyans' turn to have an attack of glorious nationalism. They demanded that all materials for the nuclear reactor and test bomb must be documented and pass through Customs, though the inspectors wouldn't know a fuel rod from a stick of Brighton Rock with a coat of paint on it. Very understandable. Customs officials have families to support. Men are enviably happy with the simplicities of Islam, Gil, especially when reinforced by bribes which make the simplicities no longer necessary.

"So the French had no objection. They needed good will all around and were experienced in the ways of North African officials. Imports to prepare the founda-

27

tions and start the erection of the reactor were quite straightforward — specialized building materials together with tons of explosives. But some of the imports for the test bomb were of course very tricky."

Rex broke off to tell me that the International Committee of Magma had often debated the theft of fissionable substances. They had planned on paper the hijacking of a transporter carrying irradiated fuel to the reprocessing plant, but decided that the threat of the stuff was limited. Let it loose, and you would have a few unpleasant deaths in a few years' time. Nothing dramatic. No public panic. Plutonium might also be obtained, but to manufacture an A-bomb from it — though there was a myth that any advanced student of nuclear physics could succeed — required deuterium, lithium, an extensive, shielded establishment and a considerable staff. When, however, they heard of U-235 going begging. . . .

"The test bomb was to be assembled on the site. The materials in themselves were not particularly sinister, apart from steel vessels containing liquids which should not be allowed out. As for plutonium, a Customs inspector could stroke a slug of it if he liked. I understand that it is harmless in that form but feels hot to the hand — which would put the fear of Allah into that brass-hatted Arab and make him a lot more amenable to leaving alone what ought to be left alone.

"The only substance which is cataclysmally explosive is, oddly enough, as safe in small packets as any other mineral. That is the pure isotope of uranium, U-235, of which the Hiroshima bomb was made. It is still the essential trigger for the H-bomb and in these days is used for little else.

28

"The French did not want that to get into the hands of Libyans, Palestinians or, say, you and me; so they hit on the ingenious idea of shipping it ostensibly for the reactor and marking the crates as graphite. It looks a little like it. You landed ten kilos of it at Blackmoor Gate. What did you think it was?"

I don't know what I answered. I had been curious, yes, but it was none of my business. Now that it was my business I felt as if I had been transferred into another personality far more important than my own. I must have mumbled something about biological warfare, for Rex replied that it was too indiscriminate, that we must always be sure that our future Lenins were left alive to exploit disorder.

"The French were too confident," he went on. "Due to transport, packing and marking on the contractor's premises, the nature of the graphite was leaked to a low level. One of our partisans — interested in quite a different project — found out and reported to the International Committee.

"About the rest the less you know the better, Gil, but I'll give you enough for you to imagine the details from your own experience. We pointed out to the Palestinians and their friends loose in Libya that the security surrounding the test bomb materials was overwhelming and that they couldn't do anything with plutonium even if they got it. So they had better concentrate on the theft of ammonite and gelignite.

"They had some rather contemptuous official help, Customs officers being allowed — possibly encouraged — to look the other way while freedom fighters acquired their wants. Our partisans among them saw to it that a case of graphite was among the loot. Transport from the docks will amuse you. It was done in a nice, new combine harvester which had cleared Customs. How useful allies can be when they haven't closely defined what they are allies of!

"The truck which should have delivered the explosives to the *Chaharazad* arrived a little late. Sugar in the tank, I believe. Our truck with the graphite arrived a little early. As simple as all that!"

"May I know where our crate is now?" I asked.

I caught myself imperceptibly hesitating over the word "our." It must have been due to surprise, as of a man who had won half a million in the pools and found himself for the first time saying "my" half million.

"In the country, Gil. Try and find it!"

"Geiger counter?"

"No, that doesn't react to alpha rays. There are other more complex devices which might detect it, but not when it is removed to London. Impossible to test every house, cellar, factory yard, bit of waste ground! It might even be in Thames mud opposite the Houses of Parliament."

"What amazes me is that the Government believed the threat and released Clotilde."

"Why wouldn't they? They know from the French that ten kilos were stolen. Anonymously we have told them by whom."

"Mentioning Magma?"

"No, not yet. We sent the warning in the name of the Palestinians."

I found it hard to steady the tone of my next question. I did not want to show too calm an acceptance of the situation or to admit an excitement which could be taken as too fanatical enthusiasm.

"And would you in fact set it off?"

"I understand it is quite easy for a nuclear technician," he replied, avoiding a direct answer. "Steel tube — an old gun barrel, for example. A large charge of U-235 at one end and a smaller charge at the other. Blow the two charges into close contact by conventional explosive, and then the high temperature and neutrons do the rest. A large and very dirty bomb. One hopes to be far enough away when the hands of the clock come around — or whatever it is. I believe our man finds a clock unscientific."

"And my London cells?"

"They would be ordered out in time. You may have noticed that none of your partisans has a family."

"Would the public be warned?"

"That's up to the Government. My own guess is that the public would be told nothing till ordered to evacuate London. Fear, Gil, fear! That alone will bring the chaos. Fear that can be revived and renewed whenever we choose."

I asked what would happen if the Government decided it was a bluff. Rex replied that Magma's plans were to prove very convincingly that it was not. Bourgeois democracy would have a better chance to obey than the Japanese were given.

July 15th

A nuclear technician, he said. Also he said that our man found a clock unscientific. So we must have got one

31

and be sure of him. More than one? Possible but unlikely. Rex never used the plural. To be able to recruit the one is a triumph, for experts in nuclear fission must be very closely vetted. When I remember colleagues of mine engaged in atomic energy research, I am sure they were all too dedicated to become politically active.

I know the man by sight. He must be the very agitated, tall, weedy-looking fellow at Blackmoor Gate. But I do not know his name or where he works. Both are going to be difficult to discover.

Why do I want to discover what is no business of mine? For the same reason, I think, that I began this diary. I am trained to collect facts and statistics and to draw from them logical conclusions, so it is second nature for me to record the few facts available. Two of those are important: the identity of the nuclear expert and the true identity of myself. Who am I? Gil to the committee and my cells. Herbert Johnson, publisher's salesman, to my neighbors and business associates. Julian Despard to myself.

My life, unlike that of most teachers, has become inseparable from what I taught. Now that thought has become action, the relevant details of my life must be examined. The mere effort of analysis, written analysis, may clarify past and present intentions.

Neither society at large nor my university approved of my lectures. I was too freely quoted and too popular among rebellious youth. My purpose was to encourage my students to question the aim and object of governing. If that aroused a desire for revolutionary action in men and women who were active idealists I was content. I must have had more influence than I believed.

His society executed Socrates for questioning. I draw no other parallel, for none of my thinking was original. What I did was to show the reasons for the discontent which exists in the western world, and what I sought to do was to turn those myriad complaints into one over-powering, reasoned resentment. Without anger the New Revolution cannot be born.

And so society executed me, not deliberately or consciously. I think it almost certain that the police believed their own evidence. I would be more hopeful of the future if they had framed me. The short-term object of Magma is to compel the State into measures of such amorality and injustice that the people revolt.

Yes, what to me was disappointing was that the prosecution honestly believed the charge of conspiracy. I was innocent. I knew nothing of the Blackpool operation which was planned and I was not a member of any cell. The friends who met at my house asked me if action was justified as a protest against the conviction of our German comrades. I replied — and I admitted it in court — that the destruction of worthless property was eminently justifiable and that loss of human life was not.

Is that my opinion now? It seems to me pusillanimous. What is a human life compared to the welfare of humanity? Avoidable starvation, avoidable injustice, the utter folly of war destroy their thousands daily. The Spanish anarchists were right when they used to say that the worse things get, the better for our world.

I, as I am, approve the blasting of the Blackpool Winter Gardens three days before the annual conference of the Conservative Party was due to be held there. That gesture of terrorism drove home our contempt for the party politicians of capitalist mass democracy. But would Julian Despard, as he was, have approved if he had known of the plan beforehand? Probably not.

The operation was nearly identical to that of the fanatical Zionists who blew up the King David Hotel in Jerusalem by delivering barrels of explosives, supposed to be beer, to the hotel cellars. That was more than thirty years ago — enough time for the trick to be forgotten. Then no warning was given. Being nationalists, they intended to kill.

Since barrels are no longer a natural delivery, our people thought at first that to repeat the trick would be folly. However, inquiries, inside information and fake telephone calls all suggested that it might work — on the pretext that many conference delegates were likely to appreciate good bitter drawn from the wood while less sophisticated socialists were content with the usual practice of drawing from tanks under pressure. The more absurd and trifling a reason, the more likely it is in our civilization to be believed. The delivery was made: two casks of explosives and four of petrol. So far Julian and Gil are united in admiration.

Warning was given and the Winter Gardens was evacuated. The police easily found a small bomb, wisely suspected that they were intended to find it, and went on searching until they discovered and triumphantly removed a suitcase with a timing device and forty pounds of gelignite. The cordon was then relaxed and public and staff permitted to return — this a good ten minutes before the time of the main explosion. To avoid disastrous loss of life young Grainger, one of the cell responsible, managed to slip into the cellar and at once fired the charge manually. There were injuries from flying glass and debris, but his was the only death. At the trial the fact of his heroism never came out; it was assumed that he blew himself up accidentally.

I have very shortly recapitulated for myself the story of the sabotage. The martyrdom of Grainger was the essential point I wished to reach in order to reconsider my reaction to it. Did I admire him? Yes. Do I now admire him? Again yes, but as an individual, not as a partisan.

There was nothing of him left. Vaporized except for a foot in a shoe. But the police had two clues. Grainger, a student of mine staying at a Blackpool hotel, was missing without a trace. A person answering his description had been seen rushing into the building ahead of the public. By the time their investigation was complete they had a cast-iron case against two of our partisans and a charge of conspiracy against me which was good enough for the jury. Fifteen years apiece for the two, five for me.

I think that I felt no bitterness. Is that true? No, it is not. It would not be true for any prisoner. What I mean is that I had no grounds for resentment. The discussions in my house had been concerned only with the theory of the New Revolution, but I could not deny my influence and was proud of it.

The judge, a little uneasy one afternoon, asked what in fact I did believe and had taught. I made matters worse for myself by giving him an honest answer. To create a passionate longing for a new order among all classes of society you must, I said, first create the maximum disorder. There are two sure methods, legal and illegal. The first, the legal, is to propagate unrest among industrial workers, especially workers in the production of energy.

"You are a Communist?" he asked me.

"No, my lord. I see no advantage whatever in exchanging capitalist democracy for state capitalism."

"I see. And the illegal weapon?"

"In theory, violence."

He wanted more and got it. Violence, I explained to him, spreads like an epidemic, becoming universal. When the disease grows intolerable, the only answer to it is the brutality of the police state, which creates still more injustice and disorder, thus bringing about the revolt of humanity and the return to a new health.

He snorted under his wig. It was the only comment open to him, for he could hardly indulge in political argument with a prisoner in the dock. I therefore closed this dialogue — in intent merciful — with a confession of faith:

"My lord, I admit that if there were an organization which could unite within itself all the Commensals of Death I should approve it."

In jail my dedication became absolute, reinforced when my escape was dangerously and devotedly effected by Magma after I had served a year. The organization of which I dreamed had noted my defiance and revealed its existence. That same day I was passed into the care of the International Committee.

My identity was changed, supported by unchallengeable documentation. The bone structure in my nose and face was damaged, and I resembled a boxer in a traveling fair until plastic surgery resurrected me as Gil. So to Jordan and North Korea for guerrilla training and, via Uruguay, home.

A job was found for me as a publisher's representative — a very convenient job which allows me to travel. So long as the orders keep coming in to the sales department my employers do not bother where I am. Gil's activities can be combined with Herbert Johnson's round of the bookshops. My cover as a good citizen is perfect. Income tax paid. Cards stamped up to date. What a farce! My real life is now to practice what I preached. Do I approve? I do.

Even if I wished to break away I could not. I cannot betray Magma without serving the rest of my sentence with years added to it for acts of sabotage in which, this time, I have indeed been engaged. And I'll bet the police can prove it, for I have been careless about fingerprints. So they must know that Julian Despard is still an active terrorist, though they can have no clue to his present name and appearance.

But do I wish to break away? Answer the question! What about Grainger, whom Julian admires but whom Gil condemns as an individual out of step? Is it conceivable to break away in this hour of undreamed-of success when at last a government is at our mercy and the epidemic about to spread over the whole globe? Rhetoric, Gil! Answer!

I answer that it is the wrong question. Gil does not wish to break away. It is Julian who is determined to oppose, to prevent, to become the stray neutron which causes fissionable material to cremate itself before the chain reaction can take place.

My reading also tells me that stray neutrons must be eliminated. I am sure Rex and the committee would agree.

July 20th

The first panic which led to the release of Clotilde seems to have died down. Since knowledge of the threat is evidently confined to the Cabinet and their top advisers, it is impossible to judge what may be going on in Whitehall. Civil Defense has not been alerted, and one can only guess what is behind the apparent lack of interest in the media. Does it mean that the Government has decided that the threat is a bluff or that front pages are fully and hysterically occupied by a couple of murders on an oil rig — more to do with matrimonial trouble at home, I think, than mysterious assassins. Magma may have had a hand in that as well. As was discovered in the last war, lies about the infidelity of wives can be more destructive of morale than a bomb down the street.

Rumors are often more effective than explosives. You can't knock twenty pence off the value of the pound or bring out a car factory on strike by acts of terrorism. My latest orders are to set rumors going in the pubs — Fleet Street pubs included — that an atom bomb has been stolen and is hidden in London. My cells have of course no idea that it is true or nearly true.

When Rex gave me my orders I could safely put a few more questions, for I seem to be marked down by the Action Committee as a man of the future. Meanwhile they need partisans, and it looks as if I am to provide them. I doubt if any other group commanders are in on the secret.

I wanted to know, as a point of security, whether the master of the ship could guess what he had delivered. Impossible, Rex replied. The master was told that it was a crate of opium from Turkey destined for America. Being a Turk himself, with the usual profound contempt for anyone who was not a Turk, he had no moral scruples about rotting American youth. An interesting point is that we do have. I used to impress it on my students that those who drug themselves for the sake of release from the established system release themselves also from the lucidity of thought which is to change the established system.

As for the helicopter pilot, he had no moral scruples either. He was convinced that he had picked up a shipment of arms for the Ulster Protestants. As a staunch upholder of the infallibility of the Free Kirk of Scotland, a few more Papists in hell were all right with him. Neither master nor pilot had any reason to connect his smuggling with Libya. They believed what they wanted to believe.

Security questions led without any discontinuity to the *Chaharazad* and its crew, who must have got ashore on the coast of Greece and out of the country unnoticed. They had been touring Epirus by car, Rex said. It was nobody's business to inquire exactly where they stayed and for how long.

"Perhaps they were camping among olives like you in Paxos."

I remarked that the voyage and its timing must have called for an experienced navigator and asked whether he was hired or one of ours.

"The committee is satisfied," Rex answered, cutting me down to size.

"And our nuclear expert knows what he is doing?"

"Yes, but from a different angle. He believes the public has forgotten what the bomb is like; they accept it as they accept earthquakes and air disasters. They read of tests in Nevada and in the Pacific and see the thing as tamable. They think that the deterrent will never be used but is essential. By God, some of them would stroll up to a man-eating lion and coo: 'Pussy, pussy, is it hungry then?' "

"That might work," I said.

"It might, given absolute fearlessness and not sheer ignorance. That's our friend's point — ignorance. Just once, he says, they should know what the firestorm is like. A hundred lives lost now will save a hundred million later."

"He's so certain nuclear war will happen?"

"That's why he is working with us. Conscience-stricken and unbalanced."

I said that he sounded as if he might take his own line, not ours.

"We thought of that, so he does not yet know where it is. When he does, his mood will be closely monitored."

"He didn't go all the way with you from Blackmoor Gate?"

"Not all the way. He wasn't far from home."

That was a useful clue. It may limit the search for him. They started off from Exmoor in the direction of Bristol.

So he does not know where it is. But U-235 cannot be loosed off without preparation. You can have too much or too little of it. The minimum is about one and a half kilos, divided into two parcels too small to start a chain reaction until they are brought into contact. Our expert has ten kilos to play with — what a phrase! — which, according to the public sources which I have consulted, is a lot less than the maximum, but enough to make an all-devastating weapon much larger than that which was dropped on Hiroshima. He must have a tricky job ahead of him with that steel tube and the firing mechanism. He and his materials have to be taken to a spot where it is safe to work. How much time does he need? A Sunday off or a fortnight's leave?

I shall have to employ one of my partisans to find and identify him. Risky, for if the committee came to hear of it they would want to know why. But the cells report only to their group commander; they may question the method of carrying out an order but not the reason for the order itself. In any case, none of them will ever suspect that Magma has the makings of an atomic bomb. I did not. I never dreamed that the release of Clotilde had anything to do with the well-publicized story of the *Chaharazad*. The Government has still given nothing away.

July 27th

The reactor at Oldbury-on-Severn is not far from Bristol and seemed the obvious place for him to be employed. But discreet surveillance has got me nowhere. Tall nuclear technicians who look as if they suffered from stomach ulcers are not uncommon, and one cannot keep up a continuous watch or start asking who does what without arousing the interest of security officers. My likeliest candidate turned out to be a water engineer, knowing little more about nuclear fission than I do.

I'm no good at this sort of investigation. An intellectual with a taste for action has not the qualities of a private eye. Only now has it occurred to me that the Action Committee would never have chosen a mere nuclear physicist in a power station. He must have had experience in weapon production and his operational center should be Aldermaston. Say he puts in so much time at Oldbury that he finds it convenient to live in or near Bristol. He might be posted to Oldbury to keep an eye on the quality of the plutonium or the management of waste. In that case he is going to visit Aldermaston fairly frequently for conferences or to report. Quickest route, whether he starts from home or Oldbury, is M4 to Newbury.

And a hell of a lot of good that is! For the police it would be child's play to check registration numbers of cars from the west leaving the M4 for Newbury and Aldermaston, but for me it's quite impossible to lay on an operation of that size. Also — which I am continually forgetting — I dare not use my cells.

July 29th

Triumph! The simplest old trick, though it's right against the rules to leave a trail of telephone calls behind. But I can imitate a vague, scholarly manner to perfection. Even if the call was monitored, it would appear too straightforward to be suspected.

For the record, here's how it went:

"Radcliffe Infirmary. Doctor [unintelligible] speaking ... Can I have a short word with Mr. ... hang on a minute ... Damn, where's his card ... A tall, thin man. Travels a lot between Oldbury and Aldermaston. It's about the irradiation of antiparasitic vaccines."

"Oh, you must mean Dr. Shallope."

"Yes, of course! Of course! Memory, my dear lady, is ..."

"He's in Aldermaston today, I'm afraid."

After a bit more pointless conversation she said, the helpful girl, that what I really wanted was the biological section of the Atomic Energy Commission and then she gave me the name and number of the right man to call.

So that was that. Shallope, having a guilty conscience, may possibly wonder if the inquiry came from some undercover police agent; but he won't think of it — to judge by the little I know of his fidgety, self-centered character. When he hears that the Radcliffe Infirmary wanted to talk to him about irradiation of vaccines, he's the sort of man to answer impatiently that it is not his specialty. At a guess the helpful girl will reply that she put the Infirmary on to the right department and he needn't bother.

He had not been long at Oldbury, for no telephone in the Bristol district was listed under his name. When I had managed to get from Directory Inquiries his number, which didn't matter, and his address, which did, I put Elise on the job. She talked to him longer than I at Blackmoor Gate and can identify him with certainty. She does not of course know that I personally want to be sure that Shallope is the right man.

I must remember what I have told her. I allowed her to believe that he was an outside expert who had been "persuaded" to assist Magma. We knew all about his contacts at his place of employment — the nature of which I did not mention — and his movements out and back. Those she need not report. I did want to know, however, how he spent his evenings and whether he was away for a night.

August 1st

Elise has identified him. He goes for brisk walks before breakfast on Clifton Down. He would. She has not been able to find out anything about his evenings because the day after her arrival he left for a short holiday in Cheltenham. She has even found out his hotel.

A most improbable spot! Has he an aged parent there? Is he taking the waters or interested in music or being shown at last where to exercise his skill? I shall cautiously follow him. The committee has to know where their group commanders are to be found, but I can get around that. Herbert Johnson has business in Oxford. That is far enough away to avoid suspicion, yet only an hour's drive from Cheltenham. I intend a dawn-to-dusk watch if it can safely be done. A big if. Some of that Korean training may be useful at last.

August 3rd

I am back at my inn earlier than I expected. Last night I settled in at Witney, a reasonable place for a country lover like Herbert Johnson to stay while he does his round of the Oxford district and twelve miles nearer to Cheltenham. It has been on the whole a successful day. How I wish I had a cell to help me! But the risk is prohibitive — quite bad enough as it is.

Shallope's hotel could not have been more convenient, or at least it seemed so at first sight early this morning with no one about. It turned out to be a former country house with extensive grounds, off the London Road and in a district which was half village, half residential suburb. After a brief inspection I left my car up an obscure lane a mile away and returned on foot to make a circuit of the place. I found that the hotel grounds had not enough cover to allow a continuous watch on the building and that the movements of gardeners and guests were likely to be incalculable.

I was tempted by a handy and climbable cedar which could be safely approached by way of the main gate and a shrubbery, but it commanded a view only of the entrance from the road and the drive, not of the hotel itself. Then I wandered past neighboring gardens and the hedgerows where town met country, looking for a secure observation post from which I could see the front door of the hotel. There wasn't one. Too many high brick walls, too much passing traffic, too many windows.

The best bet seemed to be to return to my car and drive straight into the hotel garage as if I had business there. That would give me a glimpse of the grounds from another angle. If any cell was under orders to keep an eye on Shallope, it was not one of mine and would not know my car number. I sometimes think our security is overdone, but it has unexpected advantages.

I drove in, observing on my way up the graveled drive that the garage had once been a range of stables and that under the gabled roof was an upper floor, evidently little used since the window was cobwebby and two panes were broken. Inside the garage a ladder attached to the wall led up to a trapdoor. One of the rungs had rotted through, showing that indeed the upper story was seldom or never visited. I took a quick look around and climbed up.

There was nothing in this loft but scrap iron and wisps of hay. Through one window I could see the front of the hotel and through the other a flagged terrace on the south side. I settled down to watch, though by no means at ease. If anybody did come up I was caught without any reasonable excuse for being there.

Soon after nine, Shallope came out on to the terrace, strolling back and forth with his hands behind his back. He was putting on an absentminded professor act or he may really have been lost in thought. He certainly had plenty to think about. The hotel struck me as a restful spot, with deck chairs and books much in evidence.

There was no point in keeping him under observation. The other window was more promising. On the drive was little traffic — a few visitors' cars leaving, a few trades-men's vans arriving. Two young men came in through the main gate and mysteriously became one young man without my spotting what had happened to the other. I thought that perhaps the nearest pub or public lavatory was far away and that the two had thankfully turned into the drive after seeing the convenient belt of laurels which bordered it. But the first man went on and into the hotel and the second did not reappear. It seemed possible that

my movements had been observed and that I might have
to leave an intruder unconscious on the floor of the loft
— a clumsy nuisance which would prohibit any return. I
looked for him to the left of the gate, caught a glimpse of
him nipping across an open patch of grass, and eventually spotted his legs disappearing among the green fans
of the cedar which I had rejected.

While my attention was occupied, his companion had
passed through the hotel and out on to the terrace. He
was now going down the steps with Shallope into the
garden — a young man with a fair, wispy, studentish
beard. Something about his walk was familiar; he kept his
hat on; he seemed heavily dressed for so warm a day. It
was Clotilde. Poor girl, that bra must have been most
uncomfortable! Her figure was that of a Greco-Roman
Diana, but it was not slight. The man who had so quickly
and elusively climbed the tree could now be explained.
He was one of our own partisans making sure that her
disguise still held good and that she had not been followed.

Her presence at first puzzled me but it made sense. She
had to lie low and could no longer function as a group
commander. But one must remember Magma's unvary-
ing principle of limiting top-secret information to the
least possible number. Clotilde was too valuable to be left
unemployed. If she were used to shadow Shallope and
see that there was no interference with him, it was unnecessary to let still another of our people into the secret
of his work.

She talked to Shallope for ten minutes or so and then
left. It was very possible that she had given him a time
and place, both so explicit that it was better to risk the

personal visit than to telephone. She came past the garage and I hoped to God that she would not look into it; as my former group commander she knew very well the number of Herbert Johnson's car. She passed on safely down the drive and was joined at the gate by her bodyguard.

Half an hour later Shallope left the hotel for the garage, and I heard him beneath me fussing with his car. I say fussing because he got out after he had started up and opened the hood, though there was nothing whatever wrong with the sound of the engine. He re-entered the car and again got out, slamming the door twice. Either he always double-checked non-existent faults — perhaps a built-in precaution for a man accustomed to tinkering with nuclear fission — or he had been reading in his morning paper about car bombs. My mental picture of a nervous man, easily perturbed, was confirmed. More important, I was able to note the number of his blue Cortina when he drove away.

I had to remain in my loft till the hotel and its guests were occupied with lunch and it was safe to assume that Clotilde had returned home, wherever that was, or had joined Shallope at a rendezvous. Then I drove back to the quiet lane in which I had originally left my car and sat down on warm, short turf to think and look at the map with Cheltenham spread out at my feet and the steep escarpment of the Cotswolds behind.

Some reasonable deductions could be made. The unhesitating use of the cedar meant that the hotel had been thoroughly reconnoitered beforehand — chosen for Shallope rather than by him. He was working on or had made the bomb. Where? Clotilde's visit and the holiday in Cheltenham suggested that the crate of U-235 was not far away.

However, none of that is of much help now that Herbert Johnson thinks it over again in the privacy of his bedroom after dinner. I dare not follow him. Somebody — Clotilde? — will be ordered to keep a lookout for any car sticking persistently to his tail until he is safely clear and can continue on alone. The map shows that perhaps I need not follow. That choice of a quiet hotel just below the hills suggests that he is bound for some remote spot in the Cotswolds. If he is, I can narrow down the possibilities from all Gloucestershire to a few square miles. But I can't watch the road junctions alone. Shall I call for Elise? Like so many of our women, she would die rather than talk. Deadlier than the male all right, because, I think, they want to prove that they have all the ideal ruthlessness of the male, which in fact does not exist.

August 5th

Elise turned up at Witney in the early afternoon, dark, dedicated, her gray eyes always reminding me of sheet lightning behind a cloud. I explained the position to her as if we were not happy about Shallope's movements. We wanted to know where he went when he drove away from the hotel. He might be merely visiting a relative or might be double-crossing Magma, perhaps blackmailed by someone who knew he had been involved in arms smuggling. It was essential that he should never know he was being watched.

I could see that she was surprised that I, as group commander, should be engaged on a routine job rather than one of my cell leaders, so I told her that those were my orders from the committee because my cells were mostly industrial — which was true — and my cover and experience in a rural environment much better than theirs would be.

The job, I said, might take us a day or two. The first move was to spot Shallope returning to his hotel in the evening. Starting with the assumption — which might be wrong — that he was spending his days in the Cotswolds, not in the vale, he must pass one of two road junctions on his way home: Andoversford or Seven Springs.

I sent Elise to Andoversford, which was the busier of the two. There was a chance that someone might recognize me, whether as Gil or Herbert Johnson, whereas she was unknown. I left it to her to choose the best positions and method. I took Seven Springs, safely tucked in behind a dry-stone wall. When I picked her up in the dusk we found that we had drawn a blank. No blue Cortina of the number.

We tried again this morning, changing posts. She got him at Seven Springs at 9:45. He turned sharp left at the crossroads, a move which should have brought him past me but did not; so he followed either the road to Northleach or one of the little by-roads running south. I took her off to a good and well-deserved lunch and we had another shot in the evening at spotting Shallope's return. Northleach road blank. Elise in luck again. He must have come out of a lane leading up from one of the valleys, and alongside him in the car was a youngish man with a fair, fluffy beard and a hat. Elise had done brilliantly and I told her so. When I drove her into Oxford to catch a train back to London she did not seem quite in her usual form. Too silent.

August 6th

Today Herbert Johnson took over the action from Gil — Gil, who now seems to be infected by bourgeois morality and is a traitor to his principles. I must forget Gil and remember that there was once a Julian Despard who taught what he believed to be true regardless of the consequences.

That ghost, Johnson, has contacts which have often proved useful. One of them is old Ian Roberts. He has been in love with his county since he was a boy and at one time wrote a column in the weekly paper. Landowners, the canons, the amateur historians and archaeologists, he knows all of them who are serious readers and they may borrow as well as buy from his bookshop in the shadow of Gloucester Cathedral.

What happens to cathedrals when the New Revolution is a fact? The infinite values in the earlier traditions of our ancestors must, I think, be treasured. In any case, the appreciation of beauty, though it may be inarticulate, is above all else. There can be nothing against olive groves descending to blue sea or against a glory of architecture, yet one has to analyze what is in favor. It seems that for me the New Revolution implies a New Religion. I wish I was back among my books or even in prison with time to think. The man of action must be taking a day off.

I called on Roberts. Herbert Johnson's firm is running a series of popular histories for the pig ignorant, and I intended to persuade him that he need not be ashamed to see them on his shelves. He took me into the back office for a chat and a glass of sherry. His middle-aged daughter does the selling while he attends to the buying and — though he'd be horrified at such a term — the public relations. He was impressed by the academic distinction of some of our authors and gave me a trial order. With that out of the way, I told him that I had spent a few long evenings exploring the Cotswolds and had been impressed by the timeless, well-timbered valleys around the headwaters of Colne and Churn. I said that it was like a return to the England of two hundred years ago, leading him on to tell me whatever he knew about the inhabitants.

"And earlier than just two hundred," he replied. "The Romans liked our valleys as well."

He carried on about the collapse of Roman civilization, which continued to flourish only on the country estates of the villas. Then his chins shook with a chuckle and he said that I should talk to the Reverend Sir Frederick Gammel about that. Sir Frederick believed that not only were we going the same way but that we ought to.

I said that I thought baronets who were also clergymen had pretty well disappeared since the time of Jane Austen.

"Mr. Johnson, there's a flood of houses and people all over us, but you'd be surprised how many quiet little islands are left in it. I have a valued customer on Severnside who worships the gods of Greece."

"The craze for the occult?"

"Not at all! He's protesting against it in a way. Blue skies, white marble, flowered meadows and no nonsense — that's his ideal. Founded on fallacies, just like your ideals and mine. He forgets the Mysteries and the whispers of human sacrifice that a gentleman didn't mention. And yet the farmhouse he lives in is as old as Adam, with a well-attested elemental popping in and out of the river mists. Beowulf and the Wagner stuff should be his line, but there's no accounting for some folk. Well, he's got the flowered meadows all right. You should see 'em in June! You won't believe me, Mr. Johnson, but fifty years ago I could bathe naked a mile above Wainlode and not a chance that anyone would pass!"

I saw that he was about to take me up the Severn with the salmon, whereas I wanted to get him talking about hill coverts where Shallope spent his days among foxes and badgers. That baronet in holy orders also sounded interesting. So I asked him, picking up his metaphor, what sort of island in the flood Sir Frederick was. An eccentric village parson?

"Not he! He'd set his heart on being a college chaplain, or so one of the cathedral canons told me."

"That must have been a long time ago."

"Well, he's close on seventy, or over."

Not very helpful. But Roberts went on to say that when Gammel inherited the estate of Roke's Tining along with the title he had at once turned it into a cooperative of craftsmen and workers on the land.

"An econut?"

"No. I hear his farming is quite normal and up to date. Spinning and weaving from his own wool, ironworking, thatching — those are what he's crazy about, together

53

with a wheelwright's shop and I don't know what else. He's preserving it all for the smash. Inflation, pollution, nuclear fallout, disease — all the things they threaten us with. When the New Revolution they talk about comes along he's just the man to run you up a pony trap, and I've still got the hitching post outside you can tie up to."

We had a little more half-humorous, doom-watching conversation and then he said:

"Well, you could do me a favor, Mr. Johnson, and judge for yourself if you're so interested. Take this up to him with my compliments and see if he wants it. He'll post it back to me if he doesn't."

It was a first edition of the Kelmscott Press *News from Nowhere*. I have the book now. Only when I was driving back to Witney did I realize that it would look odd to deliver a book on foot, demanding some weak explanation such as wanting exercise. But I am not risking a car down there. I want to see before I am seen.

August 8th

Yesterday I breakfasted at Northleach and left my car in the inn car park a safe six miles from Roke's Tining. My plan, so far as I had any, was to avoid approach from Cheltenham and come in from the east through largely wooded country, then looking down on Sir Frederick and his community from the high ground above the valley.

That turned out to be impossible. I could see nothing. Roke's Tining was much as an Anglo-Saxon settlement must have been — a forest clearing alongside running water. So I took to the cover, keeping off anything that looked like a path in case this was Shallope's workshop and he was guarded. I was fairly sure he would not be unless Clotilde was there monitoring his mood, as Rex had said. The general principle is never to put out sentries over, say, a bomb factory or a meeting unless something has gone badly wrong. If sentries are needed, the focal point must be so unimaginatively chosen that it should not be used at all.

The front of the house looked southeast down a narrow, wooded valley, with grass on one side of the stream and the road on the other. It was a simple Jacobean manor of Cotswold stone, warm and contenting as the Cotswold wool which had paid for it. Under the gaze of those mullioned windows I could not take the road or the meadows, and so made my way past the house along the slope. The beeches were thick on the ground, smelling of fox. Progress had to be very slow to be silent. It would be a waste of time to teach jungle movement to urban guerrillas, but if I were on the Action Committee I should like to have at my disposal a group commander who knew the drill. Well, two weeks ago they still had one in Gil, and for all I know there may be others.

When I was high on the steep side of the valley, well above the decorative chimneys of the house, I looked down into a flagged courtyard between the wings which had been invisible from the front. The far wing was wholly agricultural: barns, storeroom and a modern milking shed. The workshops appeared to be in the near wing, of which I could only see the roof. The chimneys there were industrial rather than decorative. Up the valley, closing the end of the courtyard but well away from it, was a large building, higher than the rest, which had been a tithe barn. This had a considerable chimney, above which the air danced and quivered with heat.

Somewhere a circular saw was screaming, but there was no sound of any power plant. Through the trees at the head of the valley I caught the gleam of water. It was a millpond. Sir Frederick was consistent in his doom-watching; he was running his estate from a waterwheel. He had not rejected gas for transport, however. There were two tractors in the courtyard as well as Shallope's car.

One must always have patience in the attack, over and above the patience expected by the enemy. I was pre-pared to stay where I was all day and the next if neces-sary. Patience paid off. I began to know my reverend baronet from his occasional appearances. He looked no older than the late fifties, white-haired, slender, tall, with his head thrust forward. His tweed and breeches suggested a caricature of an old-fashioned farmer, right down to leather leggings, which I had never seen before. When he was alone he had a set expression of worried vigilance, like a fine old cock with disobedient hens, and he was inclined to mutter to himself; in contact with any other person he was at once genial. I felt the geniality was in character, not the well-trained pose of our business rats.

At one o'clock I was reminded of a monastery. A bell over the arched entrance closing the courtyard rang. Out of the workshops trooped eight men and women going in to a communal lunch. No sign of Dr. Shallope. I assumed that he was somewhere inside the house. Gammel evidently put his trust in God and nuclear science or else he did not know what he had under his roof.

I had been inclined to think that he knew and approved. Now, watching him through his morning routine, I was sure that he did not. That made a considerable difference. I might be able to deliver the William Morris *News from Nowhere* when Shallope had left. But I had to be careful that neither Clotilde nor Rex nor any committee member remained behind. Nobody else was going to recognize Gil.

If Sir Frederick was not in on the secret and had been led to believe that some innocent, medieval metallurgy was being carried on in his courtyard, it was most unlikely that Clotilde would accompany Shallope right into Roke's Tining. Her voice was not deep and could not long be mistaken for a man's, nor could she take off that hat. She was able to get away with the deception when, for example, asking at a hotel desk for Dr. Shallope, but not for a whole day. Then where was she? It would make sense if she were dropped at some quiet spot to keep an eye on the lane which led out to the main road and to Cheltenham, noting any traffic which loitered or behaved at all suspiciously and ready to intervene in an emergency. The appearance of Gil where he had no right to be would certainly count as an emergency.

It was about four in the afternoon when I set out to test my theory. I reckoned that she would not be more than fifty yards from the road; farther away she could not be sure of decisive action in the event of Shallope changing his mind or of the arrival of police. Moving along the open in dead ground and crawling at intervals to the crest above the valley I could not see her, but at least I spotted where she ought to be — covering a junction of two lanes by either of which an intruder might come. The hill turf was too bare to stalk her. If she caught a glimpse of me she could slip behind any of the dry-stone walls which bounded the fields and come up for a better look.

I decided to wait, and again patience was rewarded. Soon after six a few bicycles and one car came up from Roke's Tining. Then Shallope drove past and quickly picked up Clotilde. She had shown less subtlety than I attributed to her, simply sitting in a dip by the side of the lane where surface stone had been quarried. She had an excellent view of the approaches for a quarter of a mile either way but could see nothing else.

When the car was out of sight I walked boldly down to the house. Everyone had knocked off. Monastic discipline with no overtime. I rang the bell and asked the housekeeper for Sir Frederick, saying that Ian Roberts had requested me to drop a book for him. I gave my name as plain Johns in case he should mention Herbert Johnson to Shallope. When he spoke or wrote to the bookseller, Roberts would merely think he had got the name wrong, as old men do.

No explanations were called for. Sir Frederick ushered me into his study, apparently assuming that the natural way to reach Roke's Tining was on foot. No doubt some of the members of the cooperative and the heartier visitors did so.

He wanted the Kelmscott *News from Nowhere*, saying that he had not read it since his youth but had always remembered Morris's prediction that under socialism the dustman and other laborers in hard and dirty trades would have to be paid more than the intellectual in order to attract them into the unpleasant work. He had found that prophecy impossible to believe, yet had lived to see it come true.

I replied that personally I would prefer to shift garbage and at the day's end feel that I had used my muscles, solved simple problems, and completed something of value to the community rather than work on a production line turning out needless goods, the only value of which was to make money for the producer.

"That's been put very well by the chap who was jailed for bombing politicians and escaped," he said. "What the devil was his name? My memory, Mr. Johns, is going while the rest of my old body can still praise its Maker. Despard, of course! *The Twopence-Off Syndrome*, he called it."

It was a curious sensation to find myself suddenly transformed back into Julian Despard. I knew very well that I need not fear recognition, but for the moment I was a trinity, with all parts of me in action simultaneously. It actually produced a slight feeling of nausea.

When I had pulled myself together I said — in order to open the way for more conversation — that I had read it and found it too slight and satirical for so urgent a problem. So I do. At the time of writing it I had not considered it possible to promote actively the collapse of society. I merely thought collapse desirable, and was attacking the spiritual squalor and material greed of mass democracy by way of one example which the man and woman on a London bus could understand. The proof of the final degradation of the bourgeois society is that it can be enticed by an offer of twopence off to buy an unwanted article, the whole value of which does not reach twopence apart from packaging and the costly narcotics of advertising.

Is it fair to call such an insignificant human folly the final degradation? Yet degradation it is, and insignificant it is not. "Twopence off nothing" lies at the base of all the economics of the developed world. It will be plain enough when food, warmth and work at last begin to fail.

I asked him if he had always been attracted by socialism.

"Once upon a time, Mr. Johns! Once upon a time! I now see that it is unworkable, demanding one unproductive apparatchik to every ten citizens. I therefore must call myself an anarchist."

"Bombing politicians, like your Julian Despard?"

Despard did not, but I am never sorry that the politicians thought he meant to.

"A Christian Anarchist, sir! I believe in example, not violence. You will understand if you come and see what we are doing, and perhaps you will have a meal with us afterwards."

Indeed I was anxious to understand, but to my regret I could not risk the much-wanted meal and made my excuses. Apparently several members of the cooperative lived in the house besides those whom I had seen going home. It was better not to show myself. So far I had only been seen by him and the housekeeper who opened the door.

The industrial wing was all of a hundred yards long, a third of it of the same date as the house, the rest an

addition in Cotswold stone. It was, I felt, what a place of
work should look like — a Utopian impossibility but to be
kept in mind as an ideal. Gammel opened the doors of
the empty workshops. Among the crafts was the usual
damned pottery, cabinetmaking using beech and oak
from the estate and, as Ian Roberts had said, spinning
and weaving all the way from the fleece to a finished
serge which would have stopped a knife thrust let alone
the wind. Sir Frederick told me that the product was
known to trawlermen and that he hoped for trials by the
navy.

"I am a capitalist to the extent that I provide capital,"
he said, "but my share of the profits is the same as that of
the rest of us. I consider myself as no more or less necessary than the accountant."

He led me to the large building outside the courtyard.
This was the blacksmith's shop, but far from the conventional village industry. Though on a small scale, it was
right up to date, so far as I was capable of judging, with
lathes, rollers and a lot of precision machinery for cutting
and stamping.

He explained to me that there was always a market for
small and intricate pieces which had to be specially made
by hand.

"The shop has been discovered by a wide circle, Mr.
Johns. Given exact specifications, we can forge, shape,
and temper anything small — even machine tools. It is
known to inventors that they may work here on a prototype with complete confidence in our discretion. We
sometimes have very interesting and unexpected guests!
We have one at the moment, a Dr. Shallope from the
Ministry of Defense."

The daring of it! I was and still am amazed. Yet it's logical. The most dangerous development would be if Shallope, through accident or police inquiries, were detected using a false name on his holiday. Granted that he is above suspicion, why should he not spend a couple of weeks working on some invention of his own for which Roke's Tining had all the facilities? Since he is living in a hotel and keeping his daily visits secret, he and Magma obviously hope that his presence here will not be known; but if it does become known he has a reasonable story ready.

I asked Sir Frederick what Dr. Shallope was working on.

"He has asked us all to sign the Official Secrets Act, so I am afraid I can't say more than it's a very revolutionary advance on the Stirling cycle heat engine, efficiency depending on the length of the cylinder and a special alloy used for the lining. We carry a good inventory and were ready to supply and prepare the metals he needs, but he doesn't want much from us beyond one large, simple forging and a lot of little tricky ones. A crate of his own materials was delivered here."

"And he works quite openly in the blacksmith's shop?"

"No, no, Mr. Johns! That would be too much to ask. In the house there is an extensive basement with all normal laboratory equipment. I fixed it up for myself when I was investigating the recycling of domestic sewage to edible protein. I was unsuccessful. My ideas are ahead of my time, but my chemistry is, I am amiably told, fifty years out of date. However, the problem has since been solved and gives us hope for the future."

"And the laboratory can be rented to Dr. Shallope or anyone else?"

"Well, not anyone. Certainly not anyone, Mr. Johns. But I have known Shallope for many years. We are members of the same club. You must not think I have any liking for London. To my way of thinking it is a detestable hellhole of conspicuous and unnecessary consumption, taking the lies of advertising agents as its Bible and worshiping one febrile fashion after another. The permissive society should be destroyed like Sodom, not for its permissiveness which is nothing new, but for its gullibility which is. However, one cannot lose touch with one's society, as Lot may well have said. I am no hermit, and I visit my club every second Wednesday.

"But where was I? Ah yes, Shallope! I must admit I do not like all his secrecy and special locks on the door. If he went away and left something on which ought to be off he might blow us all up. But the terms he offered were most generous and we shall be sorry to lose him. He leaves us tomorrow. The prototype is already packed for transport."

When he said good-bye to me he showed me the entrance to the basement. I wished that it had been out in the courtyard, but even if it had been and I could break in I would not know how to put this heat engine — and what heat! — out of action. That's a job on which one would hesitate to use explosives.

The Action Committee has briefed Shallope most ingeniously. My guess is that he was in actual fact known to be working on a revolutionary engine and that he may even have been backed by some endorsement from the

Ministry of Defense. Forged? Or do we have a civil servant of the necessary standing?

I had a meal of sorts at a safe distance and then slept a few hours under the stars and out of the wind. Before dawn I was in position on the open hillside with a perfect view of the road. My camouflage is worth remembering. These dry-stone walls all over the uplands can stand for years without repair, but once a storm or the horses of an enthusiastic hunt have loosened the capstones it does not take long for sheep to do the rest. When looking for Clotilde I had noticed such a gap. In the half light I scooped out a hollow for my body and reached out for earth and the lighter stones to cover me. It was a deal less comfortable than a similar job with brushwood or bamboo, but even more effective. Anyone patrolling the bare country could see at a glance that not another soul was there.

I watched the Groads Construction Company truck that we had driven to Blackmoor Gate going down to Roke's Tining. It returned in an hour with an unremarkable load which can be seen on any highway. It carried two short lengths of drainpipe lightly cased in wood and straw, with innocent ends blocked by wooden plugs just visible. The pipes might be unloaded in a builder's yard or on any site where drains were being laid. Alternatively, would anyone take special notice if a party of workmen had access to a main sewer, lowered a length of pipe, and pushed it into a disused outlet?

When the truck had driven away towards Northleach and London, Herbert Johnson shook out his clothes in the breeze, picked up his car, paid his bill at Witney, and returned home. Enough of this action in the field. I have now to think of action within the bleak uplands and tangled undergrowth of my own mind.

August 9th

I am about to kill a man. My conscience is uneasy. It now belongs to me, not to an ideal, and has become a dialogue with the self. I use this diary to reveal to me whether one side or the other is lying.

How curious that I, trained to show no mercy for the sake of man's future happiness, should be hesitant when I decide to wipe out an individual! I would not have shrunk from killing, for example, in the course of hijacking a plane to rescue a comrade.

The explosion of this bomb would infallibly bring established society to its knees, spreading such panic and horror followed by the suppression of all civil liberties that the New Revolution becomes acceptable as an alternative. Terrorism is like a painful operation to bring society back to health. Is that why I shrink from assassinating Shallope?

But the health of society is not of universal value. What is? As I try to answer that, the switchboard of the brain at once connects me to Paxos. From youth on I have experienced similar unforgettable communions when I have known a passing ecstasy which has nothing to do with human society and which is, I think, common to all animals. I am only able to describe it as surrender to a purpose, though I do not know what purpose there can be except to force me to surrender. What I receive from the switchboard is only a vivid memory of shape and color, containing neither prohibition nor encouragement nor any undertone of morality. All it conveys is: *you are a part of this.* There's a deduction to be drawn, I suppose, from that simple axiom. If I am a part, then what I carry with me into the whole affects the whole.

To hell with religion, if that can be called religion! Neutrons are what I ought to be thinking about. I am a traitor. I have made up my mind that there must be a limit to terrorism. Therefore I am bound to question whether any terrorism at all is justifiable. I shrink from killing Shallope merely because I take on myself the responsibility for cold-blooded murder. I can claim, like a hanging judge, that this is an unpleasant duty, but there is no family or club to which I can return for a glass of port and absolution.

The Roke's Tining bomb is Shallope's own baby, not a standard production; so it will be fairly primitive — not amateur, of course, but of basic simplicity and made to fit in an outer container, the drainpipe, which we have specified. It must be as difficult to ensure the separation of the two charges of U-235 as to drive them together. The foolproof, radiationproof tamping — what happens to that? Obviously it has to vanish instantaneously so that there is no risk of scattering the fissionable material before it goes critical. That means that the explosive must be special stuff, producing a very high temperature, and perhaps of little value as a propellant or for demolition.

So I cannot see anybody but Shallope himself with the knowledge to place explosive and detonators precisely, wire up, and prevent recoil. Meanwhile it must be possi-

ble without the slightest risk to crash down the drainpipe
on a pile of others or force it into a disused sewer outlet.
The final preparation therefore must be done on the
final site, sliding the bomb out of its pipe, arming it, and
sliding it back again.

No Shallope, no bomb. I think I can lay that down with
certainty.

There is an obvious alternative to killing him; but I
cannot bring myself as yet to communicate, even
anonymously, with the police and give them the facts so
far as I know them. Illogical? Possibly. I could never face
myself after such a betrayal. I must act alone. Sounds
lovely, doesn't it? But hypocrisy again! The truth is that if
the police arrest Shallope, Clotilde and the few persons
he can identify, they will at once be forced to let them go
and still will be without any clue to the present site of the
bomb. As for me, I go back to jail.

August 12th

The day before yesterday Herbert Johnson made a
business trip to Bristol, sold a few books in the morning,
and in the afternoon explored Clifton Down on foot. It
turned out to be a square mile or better of open country,
too downlike and natural to be called a park, stretching
between the Avon Gorge and the streets of Clifton and
Bristol and on the far side falling away into farmland and
suburbs. In places it vaguely reminded me of savannah
country, with trees and bushes of hawthorn sometimes
isolated, sometimes in clumps, scattered over the grassland. Plenty of people were strolling about or playing

games, but the down held them easily and I was sure that in the early morning not a tenth of them would be there.

Provided that I could make some friendly contact with Shallope, and provided the bushes gave sure cover for an instant, the thing could be done. An instant was all I needed, for I intended to use the knife silently and decisively, as I had been taught in Uruguay, so that he would be dead when I lowered him to the ground.

His flat was close to the down. Next morning I watched him leave the house and got ahead of him once I was sure of his route. He walked briskly north over the grass, his hair ruffled by the damp wind which blew up from the muddy Avon far below at the bottom of its gorge. He was wearing a heavy yellow sweater, which enabled me to keep him in sight whenever bushes intervened between us.

When he had walked nearly a mile he turned and came back across the open, where I had not a hope of attack, so I decided to meet him face to face. He would certainly recognize me, giving me a chance to enter into conversation and walk off with him into cover. It was, I must admit, an impatient, early-morning decision, for if anything went wrong he could describe me. But so he could anyway if I failed to kill him.

He behaved oddly. When he was a few yards from me he turned away towards the gorge. A slight beckoning movement at the end of the swinging arm appeared to mean that I was to follow. I suspected a trap, but it was more likely that he wished to tell me something.

I kept him in sight from a parallel course well out in the open. The patch of yellow vanished into some bushes at the edge of the gorge and did not reappear. As soon as I was sure that no one was following me or showing any interest, I strolled casually over to a point where I could see behind the cover he had chosen and at a safe distance from it.

I found that I was on the edge of a valley with a steep slope, rough and partly covered by scrub, which fell down to a road running up from the Avon to Clifton. The slope was topped by a low face of rock, eroded and easy to climb down. On the strip of turf at the bottom one was completely hidden unless somebody looked over the edge of the little cliff.

At first Shallope was nowhere to be seen; but when I peeped around a buttress of rock there he was, sitting on a ledge with a narrow terrace of turf at his feet, calmly lighting a pipe and quite obviously waiting for me. I was very willing to oblige. If he expected conversation, it could end whenever I wished in a perfect spot where his body might not be found until some pair of lovers slid down to that private and inviting terrace.

I joined him, standing well below him. Where he himself sat, comfortable as in a chair, he could be seen from a bend in the road a quarter of a mile below. He said good-morning cheerfully, without any of that jumpiness which Elise and I had noticed. Now that his job was done he was much more at ease. That offended me. He was very near to ease for ever. But at his next remark I drew back my hand from the sheathed knife hanging under my left shoulder.

"It's fortunate we met at Blackmoor Gate," he said. "I would not have led you here otherwise."

"We reckoned on that," I replied, giving nothing away.

He left his perch and sat on the strip of turf. I followed his example. To judge by the cigarette ends, a couple of paper bags and a used French letter, this idyllic spot was well known to a few connoisseurs who appreciated its privacy.

"Is this method to continue?" he asked.

"You mean meeting on the down?"

"Yes, I do."

He sounded a shade suspicious. Evidently there was something I ought to explain.

Playing for time, I said that one must always change the approach; and then, wondering what our usual method of contacting him was and how I would do it myself, I arrived at the solution. Shallope sat down on his rocky throne at a set time and anyone who wanted to talk to him had only to walk along the road below to see him.

"The yellow sweater and the same person often on the road at the same hour could attract attention, you see," I explained.

"You think there is any danger?"

"There is always danger."

"You know, I doubt if up to the present we have committed any crime."

He made that astonishing remark with such an air of worried innocence that he had another reprieve. He must at least be given time to talk.

"And when it goes off?"

"Perhaps you can tell me. You've all assured me that I needn't fuss, but I still do not see how you can keep the shipping lanes clear. A warning goes out giving the exact time and position. That can be done and I accept it. Shipping will have an hour or more to sheer off. I accept that too. But suppose a destroyer or speedboat tried to reach the spot in time? It might be practically melted."

I began to see where all this was leading.

"There's still some doubt whether the bomb will be on a raft or buoy," I said.

"Oh, a buoy! I thought that was settled. It will be broadcasting: Keep off. Keep off."

His academic voice had taken on a higher pitch in correcting me. His "Keep off" sounded very like the sea gull which might be sitting on the buoy.

I asked him if it would have the desired effect, whatever that was supposed to be. I meant the explosive effect, but he took my question in a different sense.

"I know it will. It must. People have forgotten. We nuclear physicists have made it all look so safe with our underground explosions and Pacific tests and Siberian tests. What does this generation know of Hiroshima and Nagasaki? Just a horror of war, they say. Not much worse than the firestorm in Dresden, they say. I tell you, it has to be seen. The effect of that damnable weapon has to be seen. And it will be — from the French coast, from the Southwest and from Ireland. That will show them how easily fissionable material can be acquired and how appalling is the result. Just imagine a gang of anarchists getting hold of such a bomb! Once we can exhibit its power our antinuclear forces will gain strength all over the world, even in Russia."

"The material was not very easily aquired, Dr. Shallope. It was an extremely expensive operation which cost a man's life."

"Did it indeed? I am sorry. I am very sorry. But what is a man's life when our demonstration may save millions?"

I pointed out to him that his doubts about this Atlantic operation were fully justified and that if he worked out the details for himself instead of accepting authority he would see it. The people who had studied his strong feelings and his conscience, inventing this improbable story to fit them, were not a secret antinuclear society at all, and the bomb which he had made at Roke's Tining — I threw in the name to show him how much I knew — was in fact for the use of what he called a gang of anarchists.

"Who are you? Why should I believe you?" he shouted.

I then had the difficult and unexpected task of persuading him to believe what he didn't want to believe, for I needed all the information he could give me.

The fictitious scheme of an exemplary Atlantic explosion was impressive, though I can see no way of avoiding a disastrous effect on shipping. Shallope knew that but would not admit it. I have no doubt that he had been brainwashed for months, and Rex or the bearded tiger or some foreigner of their caliber eventually produced a dozen foolscap pages of operational analysis which finally blinded our technician with unfamiliar, paramilitary techniques.

"Do you read the papers, Dr. Shallope?"

"Not every day, I am afraid."

"You remember the attempted bombing of a telephone exchange when three persons were caught and the case against them dismissed on the grounds of mistaken identity?"

"Indeed I do. A scandal! The police are getting most careless in preparing prosecutions."

"Has it occurred to you that the Government could have been afraid of retaliation if the three were found guilty?"

"Unthinkable! The Government would not be afraid of a few bombs. They have shown that very often."

"But they might be afraid of one single bomb."

"I don't believe what you are suggesting," he replied in great agitation.

"Where did your suppliers get the U-235 from?"

"Somewhere on the Continent. There are several possible sources which have caused us anxiety."

"Another item of news, Dr. Shallope!. Do you remember all the excitement about a theft of arms in Libya shipped out by a motor cruiser which subsequently disappeared?"

"Shortage of front-page drivel! One of those sensations they never follow up!"

"Why should the Libyans have publicized a theft so insignificant that it could be carried in a motor cruiser? That was your graphite, your U-235. It was brought on by ship from the Mediterranean and then, as you know, smuggled in by helicopter."

"I dare say! I dare say! But that does not mean it is in the hands of anarchists."

"The people you have met — do they strike you as belonging to a woolly antinuclear society? This cunning arrangement of meetings with you? The deadly young woman with the fuzzy beard of whom I think you have been a little afraid? The brilliant organization all the way from Libya to Roke's Tining? Doesn't it all suggest ruthlessness and long experience?"

"I admit you have me very worried, Mr. er . . ."

"The name would be false anyway, Dr. Shallope, so I shan't bother to give you one. Can that nuclear device be set off without you?"

I was sure it could not, but I gave him this one last chance for his life.

"Yes. Yes, of course. No trouble whatever. One has only to insert detonators and a timing device."

But then Clotilde or I or any trained partisan could do it. A man like Mick could talk some boghopping yobbo of the IRA into exploding the thing with no notion of what he was really setting off — a perfect example of the commensal stooging for Magma.

"I prepared it all for them," he went on. "But as they appeared so ignorant of explosives, I expected that I myself would have to make the final arrangements."

Then what was the use of killing him? I was silent for a little. I came to the conclusion, rather misty so far, that he was doomed in any case.

"Can you find out where your bomb is now?"

"I don't see how. I don't see how at all. I might tell them that I made a mistake which I wish to rectify. But I don't know how to find any of them. They come to me."

"Who are they?"

"An international circle. When I was first invited to meet them I was comforted by the fact that anxiety is not confined to this country. Very responsible people! I was most glad that protest would no longer be left to what you rightly called some woolly antinuclear society. They explained to me that pseudonyms must be used. I agreed that it was essential. I feared at first that they might want me to supply the material, but they assured me that the last thing they desired was to involve me in theft. In any case, I could not have obtained U-235, and to prepare an H-bomb single-handed is quite impossible."

Magma International at the top of its form! Kind of them to use London rather than a continental capital for their first experiment! A compliment to our efficiency, I hope.

I asked him if there was any chance that it would fail to explode.

"Not the slightest," he replied with a shade of professional pride.

"How would you dismantle it if you could?"

"Very simple. Unscrew the cylinder head. The thread goes deep, and it will take a little time. Remove the time device, detonators and charge, which should be handled with care. Then slide out Number One container. Number Two container can be left in place, since the amount of fissionable material is too small ever to become critical."

"Protective clothing?"

"For dismantling only? Quite unnecessary! Do these people intend to use the bomb on . . . on . . . well, on land?"

"They intend it as a threat. The threat may be enough

to gain such concessions as they require. If it is not — if, for example, the threat is considered a bluff — they will prove that it is not a bluff."

"Oh, my God! I must go to the police. I must go to the police at once."

"You have already done so, Dr. Shallope."

"You?"

"Special Branch is by no means bad at infiltrating subversive groups."

"But I'll get a life sentence. I deserve it for utter folly!"

"You will if you mention this meeting to your associates. If you do not, we shall do our best for you."

That, I reckoned, would keep him quiet. There was no longer any necessity to kill him. I was taking a slight risk, but at no time could I have been seen from the road and I was not expected. There was no reason why they should suspect that he had talked to anyone and interrogate him before they got rid of him.

I saw that he was doomed as soon as I spoke to him of the threat being considered a bluff. Sometimes one's own casual words accidentally illuminate a truth till then unrealized. What was his value to them any more? They had their bomb. Their immediate problem was to make the fact credible. Now they had the means. Upon the death of Shallope it was certain that Sir Frederick Gammel would at once communicate with the police. An examination of the basement at Roke's Tining must reveal to experts on what Shallope had really been working.

"Am I to continue to come here every morning at the same hour?" he asked.

I thought that over. He could not help the police with any vital information; he did not know where the bomb was hidden. His death must prove that the bomb existed, thus removing any temptation to prove it more horribly and giving me more time — more time than young Grainger ever had — to interfere with an unknown future. Meanwhile conscience could obey that amoral maxim: "Thou shalt not kill but need'st not strive officiously to keep alive."

"Yes," I said. "I think you had better."

August 13th

A restless day. I expected orders. At some point the Action Committee must need manpower. I hope they have not found it in another group. That would leave me without any clue to the final firing position.

The strike at the Hoxton Redevelopment Consortium still drags on, with the militants of the International Marxists refusing all access to the site. The men think they are striking for higher wages. The Marxists don't give a damn about wages; their attack is against the financiers who waste the resources of the people in pulling down and building up without any necessity and for the sake of profit. Since the Marxists are producing anger, discontent and a degree of social chaos, one of my industrial cells is in it up to the neck with propaganda and some money.

Ever since the day when Julian Despard decided to oppose and Gil reluctantly agreed to assist him, I have been forced, logically, to repudiate all forms of terrorism because I repudiate the most effective. That has involved deep questioning of my political beliefs. Is there a label which still fits me? I think not. Labels only help those whose sympathies are emotional rather than reasoned. Accept a label and you get your thinking done for you free of further charge on the intelligence.

For me Libertarian Communism is probably the nearest, though it makes no more economic sense than the teachings of Christ. You have eggs. I need them. I have bacon. You want it. So why don't we exchange without bothering with money and markets?

Ridiculous, of course! But in fact there is far more barter, very contented barter, than we realize among groups of friends in factories, villages, residential estates. And that is the point. Men who know one another, work together, or live together often practice Libertarian Communism unconsciously. It is in such small, devoted groups that liberty and justice can be established. It is there that tyranny can be fought, whether it comes from Marxist left or capitalist right.

I have firmly believed that only the Commensals of Death and the collapse of society can produce the seminal groups. Now I am no longer so sure. It is conceivable that Libertarian Communism could grow naturally. The stinking dung of our society is already decomposing and becoming ready for the roots.

August 15th

I was right. FAMOUS NUCLEAR SCIENTIST FOUND DEAD IN AVON GORGE — and a very accurate report beneath the headline except for that "famous," which Shallope was not. His body was found yesterday evening, exactly where we had talked, by an unfortunate boy and girl. He had been strangled about ten hours earlier with something broad like a strip of cloth. It would have been a scarf. The friendly approach and lightning attack of the former Indian thugs has, I know, been studied.

How much of what the Government now knows for certain is it going to release?

August 16th

I was at the Hoxton site and found savage police activity with no public explanation of it. All pickets were arrested and all known or suspected militants. What a howl there will be from left-wing socialists and the liberal do-gooders! My own cell had been called off the day before, but not by me. It must have been by Clotilde, whom they knew. It's odd that I should have been bypassed.

What has happened is obvious. Sir Frederick has said that Shallope's heat engine was in the shape of a drain-pipe, or packed in one when removed from Roke's Tining, so every building site is being inspected, especially Hoxton with a bitter strike in progress.

Of course the bomb is not there now, but I am sure it was and moved out before Shallope's death. We had enough influence with the militants to ensure that drain-pipes were allowed in through the gates and out again. At the beginning of the strike I was ordered to see that the pickets permitted deliveries of material, and I explained to my cell leader that the more stuff on the site and the worse it was stacked, the more chaos and overtime when the men went back. Now I understand the true reason for the order, which at the time I thought was mere ingenious mischief.

Proof will be found that the bomb was on the site even

if it demands some instrument more complex than a Geiger counter. I wish I had more than the most elementary knowledge of physics. Reference libraries are valuable, but I am sometimes beaten by the jargon and always beaten by the equations. An ability to read Plato with perfect ease does not help with alpha radiation.

Parliament and the law courts are not sitting, but the stock exchange and Fleet Street carry on and are well informed. Those who pooh-poohed our planted rumors will now be thinking twice about them. I wonder if a larger number of commuters than usual have had sudden illnesses and stayed away from the office.

August 17th

I think I am in trouble. It was folly to employ Elise on the road check just because I was so obsessed by the need for quick results. But it was no time for following my golden rule of patience.

Elise asked for a personal meeting at the same rendezvous we used when I was her cell leader. She had no right to communicate with the group commander directly, though it was I who had started it.

Shallope's death was worrying her. She wanted to know what she was to say if it ever came out that I had asked her to watch his movements. I could not see why she should suspect that my orders had been in my personal interest, not strictly in the line of duty. She seemed to be assuring me that I could count on her loyalty anyway.

I pretended not to understand, telling her that it did happen, though rarely, that a group commander picked

a member of one of his cells for a special job and that
what she knew was top secret and must not be discussed.

"There won't be any inquiry?"

"Certainly not."

"Not from Clotilde?"

"What has Clotilde got to do with it?"

"I recognized her when she was in the car with Shallope."

"You should have told me that you recognized her."

"I didn't want to upset you."

I nearly asked her why on earth it should have upset
me and then, remembering her silence when I drove her
to Oxford, it dawned on me at last what she was thinking
and why she was anxious. More coldly than I had ever
spoken to her before, I accused her of daring to believe
that I would use Magma to keep tab on the fidelity or
infidelity of my supposed mistress.

"Well, you're only human. At least I sometimes think
so," she retorted.

"And you dreamed up this fantastic idea that I killed
Shallope? Or was it Clotilde?"

"You told me you wanted to know how he spent his
evenings and whether he was away for the night."

"Have you mentioned to anyone that Clotilde had
taken to a false beard?"

"I may have done."

"Have you or haven't you?"

"Just within the cell."

"Did you say how you knew?"

"Of course not, Gil."

"Then forget the whole thing! You have enough sense

to realize that the Blackmoor Gate operation must have been planned at the highest level and that Shallope's death must be accepted without question. I was instructed to obtain certain information about him. That was all. It now appears that we could both be reprimanded for a breach of security."

So stern a superior officer was out of character for me. She must have known I was alarmed. So I was. I gave her a formal order that she was to say nothing of Shallope, Bristol and Cheltenham if asked — simply that I had told her as a joke that Clotilde after her acquittal might be going about as a man and that she repeated it without a thought.

"My own offense is mild," I went on, "but I may be censured for choosing you without a word to Mick, your cell leader."

"Why did you choose me?" she asked.

"Because you knew Shallope by sight."

That was half the truth, but I think she hoped for another half. And so we very formally parted.

I don't like it. What she has given away would be of no importance if Clotilde habitually used disguises. But the only time I have ever known her to do so was when she was monitoring Shallope. Rex also told me she did so when slipping out of the newspaper office. However, he had said nothing about a beard. I wish he had.

Clotilde considers disguise crude and infantile. By arrangement of hair and varieties of makeup she can become an attractive, grubby student with a head of flowing gold or an earnest, spectacled, sex-hungry librarian of forty-odd with a severe bun at the back. She must use a wig sometimes, because I have seen her with dark curls. That is the limit of her extraneous aids. The change of eye is of course invaluable. What I might call her business eyes are steel coils, hooded by the lids and long lashes. Yet on the street they are wide open and of appealing innocence.

The fact that one of my cells was told to clear out of Hoxton without reference to me begins to look sinister. Am I already suspected as a possible agent of Special Branch? I do not want to be sent to hell with Shallope quite so soon, even if we get there before the crowd arrives.

August 19th

A most important entry. I must have a record of everything that was said while it is fresh in my mind.

Clotilde arrived at my flat as soon as I was back from an afternoon spent with Herbert Johnson's sales manager. I mentioned to him that I might have to take a few weeks off, as my sister was very ill with no one to look after her.

"Not an official visit, Gil," Clotilde said. "I'm bored and lonely."

"Are you safe?"

"Yes. I have been given a secure flat, but I leave it as little as I can."

"All this trouble for me?" I asked, referring to the craftsmanship with which she had created from herself a very ordinary and unnoticeable woman.

Her eyes were tired. Her head was covered by a scarf tied under her chin and her hair was cleverly restrained by vulgar hair curlers. She was wearing a cheap, rather dirty summer coat. Nobody could have taken her for anything but an overworked mother of five who had just stepped out to the supermarket.

"All for you," she replied, sweeping off scarf and coat and letting loose her hair.

So that was to be the game. After long and easy collaboration, in which sex had been ignored rather than considered out of the question, some relaxation was perfectly natural. Anyone who has worked in an office alongside a woman potentially attractive but treated merely as an agreeable colleague will know how that situation may be suddenly transformed when the two meet outside the conventional environment.

I say that it was perfectly natural. What I mean is that she intended me to think so. It was to be an intimate duel in which I had one advantage. I knew what she had learned and why she had come, but she was not aware that I knew it.

However, a second advantage was all hers. I was far from sure that after long and dedicated celibacy body was going to obey brain. Impotence might be taken as a sign of guilt; so might an excitable, artificial enthusiasm. She knew my character well enough to sense any possible signal of panic. I had to be careful not to appear as the cunning but too callous spy trying to disarm the policewoman by his show of athletics.

The preliminaries on her part were surprisingly tender and hesitant. She was not at all the masterful Viking that I had expected. I called up desperate memories of one of my students whom I had passionately desired but considered too young and ivy-clinging for the risk to be taken.

Imagination failed to work. Then I remembered that Elise the day before yesterday had savagely flicked away a tear from her set face. Sheer sadism, I suppose. Yet the thought of Elise was highly approved by the wretched, offending instrument. I made love to Elise gently, long-lasting and repeated.

With my arm around Clotilde and her hair over our shoulders — I admit that once the ice had been broken I found the hair an aphrodisiac — we talked slowly and easily, as old comrades with a surprisingly new interest. Whatever approach she intended when I was relaxed and off my guard, it was now she who was softened. It is possible that all the time she had been less cynical and more genuinely fond of me than I had assumed.

"You can always ask me or Rex anything you feel you ought to know," she said.

Possibly. But only after very precise explanation of my reason for asking.

"I'm quite content so long as I know enough to act."

"A machine, Gil?"

"With specialized skills."

"It's true that when I was your group commander you never showed any curiosity. Why was Shallope killed, do you think?"

"If he was our nuclear physicist I can guess. Because he knew too much and was of no further use. If he wasn't the man, a desperate Government could have thought he was. But I don't expect to be told. My group was not engaged."

"Did you ever tell your little Elise that when I escaped from the newspaper reporters I was dressed as a young man?"

85

"I remember repeating to her what Rex told me: that you did."

"With a beard?"

"I may have invented that as a joke. It was a casual, off-duty meeting and there was no harm in telling her you were safe."

"I thought so. But the committee is nervous about all of us, Gil. The planning is intricate, and one slip here or abroad . . ."

"They haven't any doubts about me, I hope?"

"Not real doubts. And I can easily put it right. Can you let me know where you were between the fifth and the ninth of this month?"

"Yes, of course. Herbert Johnson was staying at Witney and doing the rounds of Oxford booksellers."

"Names?"

The slightest hesitation could be fatal. I wrote down the names for her. I had not been near any of them. It was a grave mistake not to have done so. I ought to have established better cover in case of trouble.

She was not so ungracious as to say that the booksellers would be visited and questioned, but I knew they would be. One or two might reply that they did not remember. Inconclusive but fairly damning. Some would be sure that I had not called recently.

The best I could hope for was that it would not occur to anyone that Witney was convenient for Gloucester as well as Oxford; if it did, Ian Roberts would talk to the casual inquirer for a quarter of an hour, saying what a nice chap I was and that he had sent me up with a book to Roke's Tining.

Clotilde left, promising to return some other evening. She won't find her Gil if she does. Even without Ian Roberts, there will be strong suspicion that I managed to identify Shallope and followed him to Roke's Tining. I might be able to talk my way out of that, but when asked why I did it I have no answer which would stand up to ruthless interrogation.

I must leave at once. It's unlikely that my movements will be watched while they are waiting for Clotilde to report. I don't know what to do. My only hope of finding out where this abomination had been hidden was to exploit the trust the committee had in me. The job is impossible alone. Fortunately Elise is safe. There's no reason for them to suspect she was in Bristol and on the Cotswold roads with me if she keeps her mouth shut.

August 21st

I have taken a room at a small boardinghouse in Ealing, dissolved among the directionless masses of an inner suburb. I feel that Ealing is an unlikely home for members of the Action Committee, though their names and addresses are known only to themselves. As for my London cells, they are scattered through north and east and I run only a remote risk of one of them crossing my path in the center of the city.

That is where I have been all day, studying faces, listening to scraps of conversation, detecting anger but as yet no anxiety. I have also tried to analyze the contents of the newspapers. They don't let the death of Shallope alone. Columns are filled with wild speculation — for example, that he was on to a method of exploding hostile weapons in their bunkers and was therefore assassinated by the KGB. Interviews with his colleagues are less sensational. He had not been directly employed on weapon production for several years and was known to be strongly opposed — in private life and common rooms — to the tactical bomb. MI5 may have considered him a very minor risk, but the extraordinary act of protest into which he had been so idealistically decoyed was beyond imagination.

I have the impression that editors-in-chief are either preparing the public for the news or encouraging the most fantastic stories because they do not want serious discussion too close to the bone. They must have been told the truth. After the release of Clotilde it would be natural for the Cabinet to have second thoughts and wonder whether the State had not surrendered to a bluff. Now there can be no more doubt. The news of Shallope's death and an immediate call from Gammel to Scotland Yard must at once have filled Roke's Tining with police and scientific experts.

Meanwhile London splutters with resentment at so much police activity. Cartoonists are having a field day with the Bowler-hatted Rabbits. The public is completely deceived by a Government statement that the danger of lead poisoning from nineteenth-century water pipes has turned out to be more grave than expected and that therefore advantage has been taken of the holiday season to measure the quantity of lead in sewers and at the same time test for radioactivity.

I am disappointed by the Prime Minister. In all his career there was never an issue he wouldn't fudge or a half lie he wouldn't tell. I don't expect him to inform the people of London that they are about to be blown to bloody hell and call for a week of prayer, but a frank and courageous warning of expected terrorist activity without a mention of nuclear fission would have been more effective. Alternatively he might have blathered — and been believed — about proposed legislation to reduce water closets to one per family for the sake of social equality.

The streets are sprinkled with police cordons and plain vans parked over manholes. The rabbits who descend from them into the sewers are not in fact bowler-hatted but boiler-suited or white-coated. Traffic is disrupted, and insult is added to injury by the reference to the holiday season. Nobody but the master spirits of Whitehall would, say the public, consider London empty in August with an extra million of sightseeing foreigners flooding in and out of the Underground on their way to monopolizing the places of amusement.

The people put in the foreground of their complaints this very minor example of bureaucratic stupidity because their hatred of the State, always extending its power on the excuse that it knows individual needs better than the individual, is unanalyzed and inarticulate. Yet there are signs of genuine anger. The vans of the rabbits have been overturned and the police attacked when they came to the rescue. The doomed city is like a trapped animal. Something is wrong. It does not know what. It can no longer believe that the hands which push in its food — with twopence off — mean well and should not be bitten.

The social chaos which must precede the New Revolution is on the way to being created already. After another week, as lies and silences, hypocrisy and lack of leadership become obvious, discontent will seethe up from the collective subconscious; and as the police state closes down on the people the Commensals of Death will strike back, appearing as the defenders of the rights of the citizen.

The next stage is to let the people know the truth. Then we shall see stark terror, crowds fighting for the available transport, and attempts to prevent by soothing words the general evacuation of the city. When it becomes known that Government, embassies and the herd of apparatchiks have already been quietly evacuated, indignation will be irrepressible.

The committee may think it enough for the present to hold the weapon in reserve and exploit the fury. I do not know. But I am sure the final holocaust will never be used to demand power nor to force acceptance of social and financial policies. Such objectives are childish and unrealistic. It will be used without threat or warning to destroy the present for the sake of the future.

We gain a clean sheet and a precious interval in which human life is no longer subordinate to the requirements of profitable production. The State will revive, due to the use of its armed forces to restore discipline, but also a still fiercer anger of the people revives. Then at last in small communities the ideals of the New Revolution begin to grow and offer an example of that content which can never be imposed from the top down, only from the bottom up.

The ideal remains my ideal, but this shortcut to it, logical as it may be, is a denial of evolution. Even if there is no purpose whatever in the Universe and human life is no more sacrosanct than that of a chicken bred for broiling, I still have faith in both. Why?

I do not know. What is the connection between young Grainger who gave his life and the setting sun in Paxos? What has the herd instinct, which I assume is responsible for our acts of self-sacrifice, to do with pantheistic ecstasy? Is it this problem which the early fathers had in mind when they formulated the ingenious conception of a triune God — a pleasant mystery to clergymen and horrifying to the literal-minded Mohammed. For me the voice which spoke to Job out of the whirlwind is more of a prohibition than the Sermon on the Mount. I must go on. I must not think it hopeless. I alone, the traitor, have inside knowledge. Not enough, but a little.

I think I should start by talking to Sir Frederick again. He is the only lead for me — as for the police. As I see it, Shallope discusses his needs with his supposed ban-the-bomb fanatics; but even they with all their contacts at home and abroad cannot lay their hands on a workshop where no curiosity will be aroused and his material can be safely delivered. Shallope himself solves the problem. He remembers or is reminded of the reverend baronet and Roke's Tining. Thereafter Magma only requires the presence of Clotilde on the spot. The choice of Clotilde is easily explained. If she is recognized and questioned the police are no nearer than they were before to identifying her political sympathies. But she must take exceptional precautions to avoid them. A more drastic change of appearance was required than mere fiddling with hair styles.

With Shallope dead and the existence of a finished bomb amply confirmed, Special Branch comes up against an absolute blank except for Gammel. I imagine that half of them insists he is guilty and must be made to talk while a more intelligent half points out that anyone who has spoken to him for an hour must know he is innocent in spite of claiming to be a Christian Anarchist. In most countries that bold confession of faith, combined with the fact that a nuclear bomb was constructed in his hospitable basement, would ensure an unpleasant week with electrodes attached to his venerable testicles. I wonder how far the police will go in a desperate situation which justifies any means.

To approach Roke's Tining is vilely dangerous. If stopped by the police, I have to establish myself as the respectable Herbert Johnson before my fingerprints are taken and I am exposed as the best catch of the season: Julian Despard. I must also consider the risk of running into some of our own people, who may not be far off. They could be expecting me if they are able to believe that I am mad enough to attempt single-handed opposition. Even if they think that I have only opted out, my death is a necessity.

August 25th

There was no reason why an honest man on a fine August day should not walk up the valley of the Churn making notes on its unparalleled domestic architecture of gray and gold. I found security beyond anything in my experience. Uniformed police were at each end of the

Roke's Tining estate; on the high ground on both sides of the wooded valley were several chaps in civilian clothes who did not seem to be doing anything agricultural. It looked impossible even to get a glimpse of house or courtyard without being questioned, and I could be sure that at the bottom of the valley were multiple activities as well organized as an ant heap. The only way to speak to the reverend baronet was to go in openly as Herbert Johnson, or rather Mr. Johns.

Though the prospect of that appalled me, there was a fair chance that Gammel and the publisher's rep could arrive at mutual trust. I was at ease with him and he with me, and we both knew it. I do seem to have the gift of warmth in human relationships. My cell, I know, was a happy team of friends. Conceit! But a desperate man is entitled to encourage himself by contemplating his own virtues.

I telephoned Ian Roberts, pretending that on my last visit I had omitted to tell him of a window display which my firm could provide. When I mentioned that I had dropped the Kelmscott *News from Nowhere* on Sir Frederick Gammel and that he had received me very courteously, I got a flood of information back with all that Gloucester knew and conjectured.

It appeared, he said, that the nuclear physicist murdered in Bristol had been working at Roke's Tining and it was believed that Sir Frederick's well-known anarchism had been anything but Christian; he was suspected of experimenting with the manufacture of bombs. Police would not answer questions. The local paper said next to nothing for fear of libel. What was true was that the

Roke's Tining road had been closed and all persons working in the colony of craftsmen had been ordered out after
interrogation. He knew one of them well — a metal-
worker who had done some machining for Shallope and
reckoned that he had been working on an atomic bomb.
Bloody nonsense! Was it likely?

"By the way," he added when he had run out of gossip,
"I had a relation of yours round here only a couple of
days ago, asking if I would let him know the next time
you called. I told him you had just been here. Edmund
Johnson his name was, and he said he was a distant cousin
of yours. He knew you worked for a firm of publishers
but not which. I gave him your business address. Hope it
was all right!"

I thanked him and asked him not to encourage the
fellow, who only wanted to borrow money.

So now the Action Committee knew for certain that I
had tracked Shallope and recognized Clotilde. I had
hoped for a longer delay. It was more urgent than ever to
trust my intuition and take the gamble of interviewing
the reverend baronet. When Roberts, returning to the
subject of Sir Frederick, said that if he himself drove a car
— which he never had — he'd go up to Roke's Tining and
tell him that he didn't believe a word of whatever he was
accused of. I replied that I would give his message if the
police would let me in.

I hired a car. The expense gave me a curious sense of
guilt, for I had gone off with a group commander's reserve of cash amounting to a couple of hundred pounds.
Although the rightful owners wanted my life a deal more
than the money, I felt an embezzler. What a profound

and human absurdity! Conscience sometimes seems to depend purely on a child's upbringing.

I was stopped by uniformed police three miles from the house and told that there was no through road. After expressing indignation and insisting that I wanted to see Sir Frederick Gammel on business I was allowed to go on. I felt more confident. After all, there must be quite a number of innocent callers, some of them coming to lend support to an old friend, as Ian Roberts had wished.

Within sight of the millpond and the blacksmith's shop I was stopped again. This time I was more nervous than on half a dozen more dangerous operations. I identified myself as Herbert Johnson, offered my business card and driving license, and gave Ian Roberts as a reference. They had a telephone by the wayside and called him up. Meanwhile I am pretty sure that I was secretly photographed. After Roberts had vouched for me I was asked why I was using a hired car. I explained that mine had broken down on the Evesham road. Where was it? I had to lie without a moment's hesitation, and I was afraid they might keep me waiting while Gloucester police confirmed my story. But they didn't. I was allowed into Roke's Tining and shown into Gammel's study by, I think, a policewoman.

Sir Frederick was surprised to see me. I said at once that Mr. Roberts, hearing he was in trouble, had asked me to come up and see if he or I could help. *News from Nowhere* was of no importance. What on earth were all the police doing?

"I am accused of allowing Dr. Shallope, whom I believe I mentioned to you, to manufacture bombs on my premises. A nuclear bomb, I suspect, though my inter-rogators have not actually said so."

"He can't have done!"

"I believe because it is incredible, Mr. Johns. I am very much afraid he did."

"Are you under arrest?"

"No. I should describe it as house arrest if such a thing were known to English law. I appear to be allowed out as far as they can see me."

I said that it was a pity and that one of my reasons for calling had been to inspect the gearing of his waterwheel again. When I had described it to an engineer friend he had said that it was impossible.

Gammel only hesitated an instant.

"We'll go and look at it. I don't think they can object. I wish you could see it working, but everything is shut down. Fortunately, Roke's Tining has a diesel generator in reserve."

As soon as we were safely out in the courtyard I warned him that his study might be bugged; if it was not, it ought to be. I had to explain the word, which was unfamiliar to him.

"I think you have rather more for me than Ian Roberts's kind message," he said when we were in the wheelhouse.

"Not here. We mustn't stay more than a minute or they'll get suspicious. Stroll back with me to somewhere in the open where we can talk."

He led me to a seat in the garden under a splendid yew where we were in full view of anyone watching us. I told him at once that I was not police or police agent or news-paperman and that I needed his help quickly.

"Shallope did construct a nuclear bomb," I said. "It was taken away from here inside an apparent drainpipe. It is now in London."

"What are you?"

"I will call myself a Libertarian Communist. That's not unlike a Christian Anarchist, but without the religion."

"There could be no profounder difference, Mr. Johns."

"You may be right, Sir Frederick. It depends what one means by religion. Outwardly I am a publisher's salesman — Herbert Johnson, not Johns. I helped to land Shallope's fissionable material without knowing what it was. If you saw his crate arrive here you will remember that it was marked as graphite. For various reasons I cannot go to the police. In any case, I could only give them the names of certain people who would get long sentences but could not help them — people who don't know anything at all about the bomb, let alone where it is. I must find out where it is hidden. What I need from you first is the name of your club, a list of members and any other information you have been able to give the police. You can tell me to go to hell or . . ."

"You are already in hell, Mr. Johnson."

"Yes."

"Is this urgent?"

"I think I have only days to disarm it or let the police do so."

"I want your true name."

"Under seal of confession, Sir Frederick."

"This is hardly a confession," he replied sternly. "Would you consider my word of honor? For several days nobody else has."

97

"I am Julian Despard."

"Thank you. I enjoyed your book. I applaud your choice of objective in Blackpool, but you took human life."

I told him how the man Grainger who died in the explosion had given his life to save others.

We were talking too long and earnestly and this was all wasted time. Before I could start questioning him we were interrupted by the policewoman, who said he was wanted in the dining room. Housekeeper, staff and colonists had all been cleared out in case one of them should guess or overhear the true reason for the invasion of experts from Scotland Yard and atomic establishments. Policewomen were providing what was practically hotel service.

Gammel accompanied me to my car. The woman and more distant colleagues watched but did not interfere. His expression was cheerful and easy. I imitated it as well as I could. No one could have guessed the urgency of our conversation.

"Can you return for a longer talk?" he asked.

"Not openly."

"I see. Yes. You must be in more dangers than one. But I presume that with your experience it is not impossible for you to approach the house at night?"

I said that I could not know till I had tried, and that if I were caught he would be hopelessly compromised.

"You could say you intended to kidnap or blackmail me. Quite believable once you are identified as J.D."

"I will do that."

"Mr. Johnson, the wiring of this house is far from

modern. I can fuse my study and bedroom lights whenever I wish and often when I don't."

"Police floodlights?"

"On the road, not in the house. And my study window will be open. There's that owl again!"

We had our backs to the car. Opposite to us, pale wings silently sweeping the lower slopes of the valley, was a fine barn owl.

"Often out in the late afternoon," Sir Frederick said. "I'm sure he's woken up by his own snoring."

His eyes and pointing hand followed the flight of the owl — up to a point. The police were also fascinated by it.

"Across the stream in the shadow of the poplar. Up that hedge to the garden. Behind the roses into the herbaceous border. Lie there and watch for a patrol, if any. Then to the study window — the one with the wisteria over it. Tap on it and the lights go out. About 11:30. Good-bye, good-bye, Mr. Johnson."

I left Roke's Tining in a rush, thankful to pass the police posts without any further inquiry about my nonexistent car broken down on the Evesham road. When I returned the hired car it appeared that the garage had in fact received an inquiry. I told them that my own car had been towed away earlier than I expected, without mentioning by whom. There was no reason why the police should start a long and exhaustive inquiry to find out whether that was true or not.

In the evening I took a bus and got off it on the Northleach road. I was intensely relieved to be on foot again: a mere nameless, numberless dot on the rolling Cotswold upland. The approach to Roke's Tining had to be from the east. The west side of its valley would be ruled out at once by the most amateur of trespassers, for after negotiating a slope of dense, second-growth woodland — a difficult and noisy job — one would arrive in the lane opposite a long stretch of high garden wall. Then access to the house had to be through the front gate or the courtyard.

The east side was far more hopeful, where beech woods ran down to a narrow strip of pasture separated from the garden only by a stream. Keeping well away from the upper line of beeches, I explored the long fields above the valley and came across a desolate knot of newspaper reporters who had tried to get at least a view of Roke's Tining and failed. I could have told them that even if one of them obtained an accurate story it would only be filed on unexplained instructions from the proprietor or editor-in-chief.

They cleared off at dusk. I had passed two or three of their cars scattered about the lanes and assumed at the time that plainclothes police had left them there. The presence of the press complicated my approach. I could not tell if any, more enterprising than the rest, had drifted into the woods unseen by me. I did not want to find myself stalking a newspaperman and ignoring genuine danger. One can calculate purposeful movement, but random movement is muddling.

In the last of the light I slipped over the dry-stone wall which separated fields from woodland and found that I was up to my knees in beech leaves which the southwest winds of many winters had piled nearly to the top of the wall. Leaves and leaf mold were underfoot. Silently I moved down through the bare Egyptian pillars of the beeches until I was somewhere above the outlet from the millpond and then followed the edge of the wood to a point opposite the house.

Gammel looking out from a lit window might have thought everything was dark. Far from it! Floodlights were at both ends of the road. Ground-floor windows were uncurtained and there was a glow over the courtyard. The strip of open pasture and the stream, both of which I had to cross, were damnably naked under the moon and a clear sky. I could clearly see two police patrolling my side of the stream, over which was a footbridge mercilessly lit up. At the northern end of their beat they were very close, and at the southern near enough to spot me crossing the open.

I tried to follow the edge of the wood and reach a point beyond their regular beat, but there the thick growth of ash and hazel which I had easily managed in daylight could no longer be tackled soundlessly. The police were right not to bother with it. So I had to stay among the more open beeches, where at least I was invisible. Settled into a cradle of roots, I timed and watched the movements of the patrol. Half an hour's patience produced no solution. I should have no trouble in escaping if seen in the open, but to try to reach Gammel's study window was asking for trouble.

It seemed to me that I now heard a second patrol coming down obliquely from the wall. Listening to faint and distant shufflings, I concluded that there was only one man; he might be one of the news hawks hoping for a scoop, but whatever he was I had to be sure.

I waited just off the line of the cautious footsteps, glimpsing first a moving darkness and then getting a clearer view of the man as he slipped across a moonlit clearing instead of going around it. Dear Mick, he still had a lot to learn!

Of course they had chosen him because we had worked so long together in the cell which he had taken over from me; he would recognize me anywhere and in any light. I let him go on until he came to the thicker undergrowth which would stop him and meanwhile gave some thought to a situation which I had considered very unlikely, though taking reasonable precautions.

It had never occurred to them that Herbert Johnson had driven boldly in, risking awkward questions and identification as Julian Despard; they reckoned that if I intended to stick my nose into Roke's Tining I would arrive from the east in some such way as I had. However, that was only an intelligent deduction from my known tastes and training, quite insufficient to launch the operation against me unless I was actually seen. I must have been. It could be that Rex had a partisan posted among those roving reporters or in an apparently empty car which I had approached too carelessly. Also it was probable that, once I had crossed the wall, someone would be posted to stop me from breaking out if I scented danger. I was bound to leave the wood at the top rather than risk the lights and the police in the valley.

Why they believed I would come to Roke's Tining at all was uncertain. Gammel could tell me nothing which I did not already know. Or could he? Or did they think I had something of vital importance to tell the police? But in that case I would surely report at some secret interview in London, not here.

For the moment answers to those questions could wait. The essential thing was to guess what Mick's orders were. I doubted whether he would ever agree to kill me, even if assured that his group commander had defected and was dangerous. That suggested that there must be someone else with him to do the job, which had to be finished crisply, without firing a shot or giving me time to yell. A professional was needed. He could hardly get near enough for the thuggery which killed Shallope or the syringe. Arrow loosed at short range? Blowpipe? All the methods expounded during training, even the use of the long spear from cover, ran through my mind. But before any action Mick must identify me and report. If I allowed him to do so he could lead me to his companion.

To judge from their behavior, neither of them realized that he might become the hunted rather than the hunter, confident that I would not attract police by a shot, confident too that I was unarmed if running true to form. My cell knew that on principle I never carried a gun and were divided between admiration and disapproval; but I had never let any of them detect the soft-sheathed gaucho knife that rests under my left shoulder on all occasions when it might be needed. My choice of weapon is deliberate. I cherish it and sometimes test the blade by shaving with it. It makes aggression at a distance impossible and yet assures efficient personal defense if attacked or too casually arrested.

I sat down on the edge of the moonlit clearing to wait for Mick's return from the impassable bit of thicket and to allow him a clear view of me, backing my hunch that he must have been ordered not to disturb the silence and that he would not be chosen as the actual assassin. A third comforting thought was that anyway he was a lousy shot. But I admit that I did not enjoy sitting there and offering him a sight of my head.

As soon as he was sure he turned away from the clearing and went up the hill, now very slowly and taking the utmost care. I doubt if his footsteps would have been audible if I had not been expecting them. I followed him at a safe distance, stopping when he stopped, until the bank of leaves which shrouded the wall was faintly in sight.

Mick disappeared behind a group of three smooth boles, too far away for me to hear if there was whispering, but everything pointed to it. After half a minute he returned cautiously over the leaf mold more or less on the route by which he had come. I waited for his companion. He slipped out at an angle and I could only see that he was a big, heavy man with a belly who moved as lightly as a boxer — a far more formidable opponent than Mick.

Padding down on a parallel course I caught sight of him at frequent intervals. When he was above and close to the clearing I saw him stop, take from his pocket a corked phial, pick out a dart with a pair of tweezers, and load an air pistol. To paralyze or kill? Whichever it was, the effect of the dart had to be nearly instantaneous, working so fast when it pierced the skin that the victim keeled over while still wondering whether the prick was caused by thorn or insect.

Somewhere he had had more training than that of an urban guerrilla. He waited near the edge of the long strip of pasture in the valley bottom, summing up for himself the lights, the patrol and the general activity. He must have seen, as I had, that the only hope of reaching Roke's Tining was to wait and wait for a chance opportunity. Waiting, therefore, was what I was doing when Mick spotted me.

He took up his position some ten yards back from the open. I couldn't see him since he had a tree trunk behind him, but I knew which tree. Escape never occurred to me. I was obsessed by the necessity of keeping my appointment with Gammel and gorged with an absolute loathing of this murderer without any creed, public or personal.

Everything about him — expression, build, method — cried out that he was not one of our partisans but a hired assassin killing for money, a spiritual monstrosity. Attack the State, yes. Accept loss of life if it cannot be avoided, yes. And yes, exposure and execution of the infiltrator. But it fouled Magma to recruit a butcher from the terror bank as if we were drug-runners or a crooked industrial Mafia. Looking back on that night I detect some hypocrisy in my indignation, but it was real enough at the time.

I wanted my more honest Mick to be well away, but I had no idea where he was. He might be more or less in line with us and advancing just inside the trees to drive me towards his companion, or above me, hoping to close in if I were seen or heard climbing up the wood. All was dead silent, so I decided that the dog should be allowed to look at the rabbit again. I left the killer to go on contemplating nothing, reached the lower end of the clearing, and deliberately tripped. That brought Mick out of hiding at once and fixed him on the spot.

Then downhill once more. I was aiming for the last rank of the trees rather beyond the point where my enemy was, and I was too confident. I overlooked the fact that all this time I had been guided by their movements rather than by remembering small details of the ground. There were few. I could see the limit of the wood from quite a distance inside it because of the lights in the valley. I could feel the angle of slope and be sure where the clearing was, but to recognize a pattern of tree trunks in darkness irregularly stippled by patches and stripes of moonlight was difficult.

I chose the wrong clump, and my mistake was made still more deadly by one of those long, low beech branches searching for light. Instead of going around it I ducked under it. When I raised my head he was close enough to spot the movement of the pale face. I hurled myself sideways and heard the *phut* of the pistol and the tap of the dart as it hit the branch. Then he was on me and I went down under his weight. My only chance was the old possum trick of limpness. My right hand was already on the hilt and I had the sense to cross the other arm over it as I fell, as if hugging myself in a position of utter terror. He never bothered to see what either helpless hand was doing and picked up the wretched bundle by the collar, about to strangle it or deliver a knockout blow which would give him time to reload at leisure.

I couldn't breathe and held what breath I had while I smoothly, almost lovingly, inserted the knife till I felt the muscular resistance of the heart, then cut downwards to the tight waistband which reminded me that I might have to pick up and dispose of whatever it let loose. A savage reaction, panting with fear, pain and fury. I could understand those Moslem primitives who stuff the victim's mouth with his penis.

He had only time to utter a high-pitched, half-voiced gasp. The police patrol heard it and turned around but made no move. They may have taken it for the strangled hoot of that owl with his mouth full, or for any of the tremulous mealtime comments of fox or badger to which they no longer paid attention. There was no noise at all as I lowered his body to the leaves.

I stood back until the beat of my heart had slowed and the animal was again relaxed. I found unfathomable Mick on the far side of the moonlit glade, anxiously listening either for me or for a repetition of the curious sound he had heard. From the cover of two overlapping trunks behind him I asked:

"Your orders are to kill me, Mick?"

He swung around. The voice was very close but he could see nothing.

I told him to go forward into the clearing and drop his gun. He obeyed without a word, still not knowing where I was. To my surprise he was not armed.

"Who was the man with you?"

"He's foreign. That's all I know."

"Was foreign, Mick. Go down and look and keep just as silent as you have. You did as well as could be expected without more training."

He started down while I kept behind him and directed him to the body.

"You devil!" he whispered.

107

"I've heard you say that before. Yet I'd never killed anyone then."

"Did you have to do that?"

"Unless I wanted to be killed myself. What were your orders?"

"Committee orders. Direct. They said you had buggered off and might be dangerous. Nervous strain, like. We were to find you and bring you in quietly."

That at least is the gist of what he told me at greater length and incoherently.

So as to stun him with still more surprise, I asked him if he knew who I really was.

"Herbert Johnson."

"I am Julian Despard. Is it likely he would become a police informer? And from all you know of Gil, would he betray his cell or his group?"

"What's happened?"

"I'll tell you. But we must get rid of this. What were you going to do with me?"

"Carry you away. I didn't know exactly. This one did, and the two up there."

"Where are they?"

"In a car about a mile away."

"And you were going to carry an unconscious man through this wood, over the wall and a mile across country without being seen or heard?"

"This place — what is it? I didn't know it would be crawling with cops."

"Well, now you do. They led you up the garden path, Mick. My body was to be left here."

"But it would be found."

"I doubt if that would matter. A dead Despard adds to mystery and fear. But I don't want to leave this one. Put that stuff back, take off his coat, and button it round him lower down!"

He did what he was told. When the patrol was at the far end of its beat we carried the body up to the bank of leaves and buried it deep. It's unlikely to be found for a week or two and by then, unless I can alter the future, courts and police will be only a turbulence. God, how desirable! But not at that atrocious and intolerable cost.

Mick looked me over with his untidy half grin and said he couldn't see much sign of the nervous strain.

"I might play your game with you if you'd tell me the rules," he added.

"Sit down and I will. It starts from Blackmoor Gate. I didn't know any more then than you do now."

He only interrupted when I came to my interview with Shallope.

"So you didn't kill him?" he asked.

"No. He was killed the next day. It was well calculated — the best way of convincing the Government that the bomb existed and we had it."

Mick's reaction was very like my own. The objective for which we had suffered and fought and dreamed and destroyed was in sight, but it should come in its own time.

"It's too . . . well, too sudden for me," he said. "I can't accept this weapon but I can't argue why not. I don't know what you mean by your purpose. Arrangement in blue and olive by Gil and bloody God! There's no object whatever in life beyond what we pack into it and you know it. It's a nasty chemical accident. But whatever the hell you did mean, this is *my* revolt — your voice, the night and all the poor devils lost in night like that Grainger you've reminded me of. You split this bastard up for yourself, Gil, but I know you well enough to be sure you killed him for our beliefs, yours and mine. What'll I tell them when I go back?"

"How did you get here?"

"Hung around with the newspaper blokes."

"Then just say that you did see someone enter the wood and followed. But you never saw him again and couldn't find out whether he was Gil or not."

"And the late Guts?"

"You lost touch in the dark and waited but never heard a thing. So you cleared off before it was light and couldn't find the car."

"It's a fact I couldn't, alone."

"Bad organization and you can say so."

"Wouldn't it be better to tell them I heard him cry for help?"

"Too hard to explain. Let it stay a mystery till the police find the body, if they ever do. But you can cry for help yourself now."

"What for?"

"To draw off the patrol and give me a chance to reach Sir Frederick."

He thought that over and came up with a far better suggestion.

"I've got a torch on me. Suppose I start flashing it on the ground near enough for the patrol to see the fairy lights. That'll bring 'em into the wood after me."

"Are you sure you can get clear?"

"How much noise did I make?"

"Almost none except when you were in the leaves here."

"Well then! Where shall I find you, Gil?"

"I'm taking no chances. But I'll be in London and I know where to find you."

When the patrol had reached the millpond and turned back on their beat, Mick slipped away ahead of them. From where I was I could not see the pool of light flickering over the ground in and among the tree roots, but its effect on the police was immediate. As soon as I heard them charging after the will-o'-the-wisp uphill, I raced across the grass and into the pitch-dark stream under the poplars. There I dipped coat and right sleeve into the water to wash out or at least disguise the bloodstains.

Gammel had merely said "up the hedge," without specifying which side of it. It had to be the near side. To reach the far side I must pass across a semicircle of lawn at the foot of the hedge shining in a naked light over the footbridge. It was a high wall of yew, shadowed from the moon, along which I crawled and walked without fear of detection; but it was thick enough to stop a charging bull and impassable, so facing me with an awkward problem, for it ended not at any rosebed or herbaceous border but slap up against a balustraded terrace — yards and yards of gleaming white flagstones flooded with light from two open French windows.

Inside the room — probably the communal dining room — six men and two women were seated with their papers at a polished table, half of them facing the terrace. I gathered that it was an important and contentious conference of nuclear scientists, but the little I overheard was too unintelligible to be of interest. I dared not climb the balustrade and get around the yew hedge, nor was I going to risk returning to the stream and passing round the lower end of the hedge under the light over the bridge. But the power of quick decision breeds on itself. Still excited by my discordant efforts of successful violence and peaceful persuasion, I took a chance which I would never have considered in any cold, preliminary planning and called out in the firm voice of a passing security officer:

"Draw the curtains if you please, gentlemen!"

It worked. Somebody got up and drew them. I was able to nip up and down the balustrade, around the end of the hedge, into the rosebed, and thence behind tall delphiniums till I was opposite the open study window. I need not have bothered to wash in the stream. Gammel's eyes would only notice on me the imperial purple of his Cotswold earth with a sprinkling of well-rotted manure.

I tapped on the window and crouched beneath it. A second later all the house lights went out. Voices at varying distances joined in an oratorio of curses, leaving no doubt of a Roke's Tining swarming even at near midnight with busy investigators. We ourselves preserved absolute silence. Gammel quickly brushed off the loose earth from the sill, shut the window, led me into the adjoining bedroom, and motioned me to get under the bed.

They did not take long to change the fuse. As soon as there was light again he went to work on the remaining traces of my passage and had barely finished when a security officer came in to find him sitting at his table with an open book. I heard Sir Frederick apologizing profusely for his carelessness and showing with a display of senile inefficiency exactly what he had done — which of course fused the lights again.

The security officer flashed a torch around the bedroom and cleared off. After that we were left in peace. Gammel had taken to heart my warning that his study might be bugged and took no chances even with the bedroom. He lay on the floor with his head under the valance of the bed and close to mine. A curious position for a vital interview.

I told him that I had evaded the police but had been seen above the valley by unknown, possibly interested persons. That was all he needed to know. He was a little cold to start with, no doubt wondering why on earth he had accepted my integrity on the strength of so short a talk together.

"And so, Mr. Johnson, you believe you can do better than the police?"

"I know I can, since I have more knowledge of the background than they have."

"Then you should share your knowledge with them at whatever risk to yourself."

I replied that I was very willing to share and could do so anonymously with little risk to myself.

"Impulse sent me to you, Sir Frederick, and impulse made you receive me kindly. Believe me, we are both right."

"We are," he said more warmly. "Yes, we are. But I assure you the police know everything — how the bomb was constructed, how it was packed. Everything!"

"But not where it is."

"Why do you think I can help in that?"

"Because my former associates are so anxious to prevent my talking to you."

"Then you had better put questions to me, Mr. Johnson — more sympathetically than the police, I hope. I will do my best, but I am so weary of answering: 'I don't know.' "

"Can you remember who first introduced you to Shallope?"

"The police kept on after that. I could only tell them I had known him for years. Off and on. At the club. Never, I think, anywhere else till he turned up here with his proposal."

When he said he had a list of members for me, I hoped to recognize one of them as belonging to Magma, though I might not know his cover name. But while I was still explaining that the list could be more useful to me than the police I saw the futility of it. I should be involved in endless and dangerous watching of the club's front door just for the unlikely coincidence of spotting one of the Action Committee such as Rex.

I was silent for a bit, thinking of what other useful questions I could put, and then remembered how weeks earlier I had wondered about the identity of the navigator from Benghazi to Paxos.

"Have you a friend — or someone who knows all about Roke's Tining — who is a naval officer or connected with the sea?"

"Naturally I have in the course of a long life. Mostly retired now. And there are many visitors to Roke's Tining whose names I regrettably forget."

"Look back some months! Anyone connected with the sea and interested in your experiment in communal living?"

"Young Mallant. But he's no good to you. I knew his father, Canon Mallant, intimately. A strong character but carrying his faith to extremes. He could not be dissuaded from speaking with tongues. The archdeacon, I remember, commented that alcohol was more recognizable than Aramaic."

"His son takes after him?"

"An original character, yes, but not the type to be a churchgoer. I knew him well in his early twenties, and some months ago we lunched together. He is an ethnologist. Quite distinguished, I believe."

"Can you remember whether he invited you or you invited him?"

"I invited him. He sent me a charming Christmas card, hoping that we could meet again after so many years, and I asked him to lunch with me. He was most interested in our self-sufficient community."

"And he's a navigator?"

"I should think he must be. He spent some time in the Philippines studying island societies. And he has a side interest in ancient history. The migration of the Etruscans. The foundation of Greek colonies. How many men were needed? What craftsmen, cattle, women, builders? How many voyages went to make a viable settlement?"

"I suppose he must have followed their routes."

"Yes, I am sure he mentioned that, though we talked mainly about his father. He also drew me out on the subject of Christian Anarchism and I fear I talked far too long about my own experiments."

"Can you describe him to me, Sir Frederick?"

"Let me see, now! Black, straight hair inclined to fall over his forehead. Lank. Lank, I believe, is the word. A neat beard. Quite remarkable eyes. Tall. When I saw him stand up after lunch I thought to myself what a splendid human animal he was. A natural leader, Mr. Johnson! Such a pity that men of that type do not enter politics!"

There was my tiger man described to the life. And it was no wonder that the committee wanted to keep me apart from the reverend baronet. I and I alone had been present in Paxos and at Blackmoor Gate. I had asked Rex about the navigator and been snubbed, and I see looking back at this diary — an example of its value — that I also mentioned the precision of the navigation to Clotilde, who had been at once and very cleverly evasive.

I asked Sir Frederick if he knew Mallant's address. He retired from under the bed and I heard him rummaging among papers in his study.

"There it is, some chambers in Hunter Street owned or controlled by the Museum, I think. But you surely do not believe . . . dear, dear me, it is just possible, just remotely, but not in any — shall we say? — executive capacity. Sympathetic he might have been. Should I give his name to the police, do you think?"

I replied that if Mallant were called in for questioning there were three possibilities. He might be released with apologies, for there was no evidence against him but mine. If my evidence was accepted and he was arrested, he would be set free by the blackmail of the bomb. Alternatively, it might be immediately exploded if there was a chance of discovery.

116

"Personally, I should not let him go and I should choose for him a London prison," Gammel said stoutly.

"It's not a question of his guilt, Sir Frederick, but of what he must know. I can only get a line on that if he is free to move."

I might have added that the odds were strongly against my being alive to get it, but I did not wish to alarm him. I underestimated him there. He had worked it out for himself.

"I think you have not yet appreciated that in some circumstances an old man can be a useful ally, Mr. Johnson. It does not matter to him whether he lives on for five days or five years. Time runs so swiftly."

A rare point of view. I imagine it owed more to the reverend than to the baronet. Both sides of him appeared more formidable every minute.

"If you should need me I shall be at the club next Wednesday," he went on. "The police have no objection. Indeed they cannot have, since I have not yet been charged with anything."

He did not fully realize that whether innocent or guilty he was the only clue the police had. It was probable, I told him, that he would find in the club porter's box a temporary assistant whose true duty would be known only to the secretary and Special Branch. He could assume that his telephone calls, if any, would be monitored, that his outgoing mail would be intercepted, and letters received would be read. Quite apart from these attentions, his club was sure to be watched by a Magma cell in the hope that I might visit him there. I gave him my Ealing address and the name I was using and explained that he could safely write to me provided he was not seen to post the letter.

"You mean a special collection might be made just because I was seen to post a letter in the box?"

He was no longer indignant, only disconcerted by his own importance. He asked me again if he should not give Mallant's name to the police, and I repeated that it was far too dangerous unless we could also give them the precise location of the bomb.

"Who is in charge here at Roke's Tining?"

"A chief superintendent of what they call Special Branch. He has questioned me at very great length together with an assistant commissioner named Farquhar, a very courteous gentleman but persistent. I believe him to be a Presbyterian."

I longed to ask why and what difference it made, but it was now time to consider how I was to leave the house. Could he suggest any better route?

"I have been busy since you called this morning and have been able to arrange it with our cabinetmaker. He has nearly completed a dining room suite and I obtained permission for him to take it away and finish it. The sideboard is a massive piece and will hold you. I have instructed him to load it last, to make no comment on the weight, and to see that the doors face the back of the van."

"But can he be trusted?"

"The whole of my community, Mr. Johnson, is founded upon mutual trust. Without it there can be no society of this or any other kind."

"How am I to get to the carpenter's shop?"

"That I worked out this evening. The courtyard is lit

but not guarded. Now if you would be good enough to follow me quietly to my bathroom . . ."

Mutual trust was fine, but I doubted whether Sir Frederick had sufficient experience of criminality. I still underrated him.

"You must remember," he said, "that for the last few days I have been living in what is practically a police station. I know their movements."

The passage outside his study was lit but safe enough so long as nobody suddenly appeared from any of the doors. The bathroom — evidently converted from a small but stately private boudoir — had a double casement window. He left the light on long enough to avoid suspicion, then switched it off and showed me that the window opened on to a shadowed corner of the courtyard.

"We will wait till the outside patrol has passed between the wings. You can then go through and enter the third door on the right, which is open."

"And if I am seen walking there?"

"Step out with confidence, Mr. Johnson, and it will not matter. I have so many guests. Should you be glimpsed by a plainclothes officer off duty — which is unlikely since their rooms face the road — he will take you for one of the scientists and vice versa."

To my surprise — then and now — my exit from Roke's Tining was as private as my arrival. The sideboard was commodious. In the morning I felt it lifted and loaded. Twenty minutes later we stopped at a red light with no traffic behind. I slipped over the tailboard and found myself on the outskirts of Cirencester. Six hours later, by bus and train, I was back in Ealing and at peace.

119

Well, peace I will not say; but given a definite objective, however unattainable, one can rest temporarily instead of fretting with frustration.

August 27th

I read my last entry with disgust. I see a ruthless killer and paranoiac puffed up with self-satisfaction because he was trained to move cautiously in woodland — no more a matter for pride than if he were trained to program a computer. And now this paragon of action is so helpless, so unenterprising that he sits safe on his bottom in his Ealing boardinghouse when he should be out and resolute.

Mood! Mood! How many contradictory pictures of himself can a man survey through the viewfinder of self-esteem? If I could see my way ahead I should call this inactivity patience and give myself a pat on the back. I sympathize with the Prime Minister. He is certain that somewhere in London is an exceptionally dirty A-bomb and cannot find out where. He does not know — and nor do I — whether it will be used for blackmail or, coldly, without any pretext at all, to trigger the destruction of the hateful consumer society. All he can do is to sit, to wait for police reports, and to lie.

I too wait for my police report in the shape of Mick, who now knows where he can find me. A calculated risk, but I cannot work alone. In fact I am even surer of him than in old days. Disillusion has left him empty and only loyalty to me can fill the gap. His story was accepted, but they are worried that the expert from the terror bank has never returned. He is known as Vladimir and should have been flown back to Germany.

I have set Mick on the trail of Mallant. It should be easy to shadow that distinguished ethnologist, who is confident that he is unsuspected. To judge by what Shallope told me, I think he is responsible to the International Committee for this weapon and its use.

Tomorrow is Wednesday and my reverend baronet will be in London. The day after I may have some word from him. I don't really need him at the moment except for personal morale. He is so enviably sure of the difference between right and wrong.

August 29th

At last news and more news. How is it that a period of blank, blind days is so often succeeded by a whole spate of events? Is there some minor and divine executive in charge of this world who takes a week off and then deals with the backlog, inspiring one of his servants like the reverend baronet to issue an order? And an order it is! Here is what I get this morning:

"I fear Roke's Tining has more than ever become an annex of Scotland Yard. A fox and subsequently our resident population of carrion crows have revealed a body most foully murdered. I have been asked if I can identify it, which I am unable to do. I understand from one of the more friendly of my visitors that he is believed to be a foreigner and that on the night of the twenty-second lights were seen in and among the beeches above the house.

"I find myself in something of a quandary and must demand your immediate advice. I shall expect you the day after tomorrow in the midafternoon. You may rest assured that I have devoted earnest thought to the question of a rendezvous. You will ascend Pen Hill, and when I see you there I will indicate your subsequent movements. I am still permitted to take mild exercise unobserved."

I don't like it, but I must obey. Gammel is probably right in claiming that mild exercise is not supervised. By this time Special Branch must surely have summed him up. Eccentric certainly, but a man abhorring violence. I shall have to tell him the truth and hope that under the circumstances murder will appear to him no more or less permissible than in war.

When I left the stale neutrality of my boardinghouse for lunch, I observed that Mick was following me at a discreet distance and led him into Gunnersbury Park where we could talk at leisure. He has spotted an oddity in Mallant's morning movements.

He leaves his Hunter Street flat at about nine o'clock for the British Museum. The obvious and quickest way of getting from one to the other is to walk, but he doesn't. He takes the Underground at King's Cross and alights at the next station, Russell Square. Now the distance from Hunter Street to King's Cross is about the same as that from Hunter Street to the Museum. So why take the Underground? He would gain nothing even if it was pouring rain.

Had Mick noticed anything unnatural about his route? No, it was fairly direct. Mallant might take the first or second turning after leaving his flat, but he always went through Argyll Square.

I used to know Argyll Square when I was attending a postgraduate course at London University. Its architecture suggested that it was there before the great railway stations of the capital, but the Georgian fronts had become vulgarized by the crowded signs of useful little hotels with pleasant bedrooms, a minimum of bathrooms and unspeakable food for any traveler taking more than bed and breakfast.

It then had the remains of a pleasant garden in the center. I asked Mick what it was like now, for it might be that Mallant preferred to start his day with a few trees and flowers.

"Nothing much," Mick replied. "More of a playground than a garden."

"Is he always on the same side of the square?"

"Yes, he follows the two hotel sides, but he can always see the others across the garden."

Mick was sure that he had not been trailed or noticed. Ordinary care would be enough if Mallant conforms to the rule of never using a shadow when there is no need. However, this tailing was far too risky. Mallant checked the lorry with Mick at Blackmoor Gate and would not forget a face.

If I were in his position — and the care given to my training suggests that I was being groomed as a possible adjutant or successor — I should want to keep an eye on the weapon, perhaps daily. That may be what Mallant was doing. I told Mick to take a front room in one of the many hotels and watch from there, using his imagination and not rejecting any theory, however wild. He said he could well run into someone who knew him, which might lead to awkward questions. The cheap hotels, conveniently close to St. Pancras and King's Cross, were for thrifty visitors from the North — foremen, engineers, salesmen, shop stewards.

"Can I order Elise to do it?" he asked.

"What have you told her?"

"Nothing. There'll be no need to. After all, I'm her cell leader and can tell her to watch out for the tiger man and report every movement she can see from her bedroom window."

"Suppose your whole cell is ordered out of London?"

"Well, the order comes through me. She doesn't have to tell anyone else where she has been and she should not."

I agreed to that. It was a step in the right direction, for eventually I want Elise on my side.

"I think you had better give her the impression that Magma is protecting Mallant, but don't ever let her know his name. Tell her to keep her eyes open for inspection of drains or taking up the road, any rebuilding or conversion jobs, any delivery vans waiting and not delivering, any sort of pattern or anything out of the ordinary."

I left it at that. The time for anxiety will be when Mallant leaves London.

The Roke's Tining murder is in the evening papers. Not headlined. Just a mention without gory details. Police must have asked editors for extreme discretion. I hoped the body would remain concealed much longer. Now the committee will know that I am an active opponent and I must expect a determined effort to find and silence me.

August 31st — and 4 A.M. damnit!

I have trouble sleeping, for it seems a waste of time. How well I slept in jail when there was nothing else to do! Well, it's better to record the curious yesterday than to toss and turn.

I took an early train to Stroud and walked the remaining ten miles along the high edge of the Cotswolds. These forced, invigorating marches are their own reward. Despair was impossible when striding over the windswept, short turf and looking down on the green valley of the Severn, with the silver river itself shining at the bends where it flowed away from me, and the tower of Gloucester Cathedral so small in the distance, yet dominating all the lush land between Cotswold and the cloudy ranges of Wales. I had the impression of two worlds, each with its own time — the fast clock of my physical body pressing towards its limited objective and the steady state of a distant reality spread out at my feet but only attainable through a peace consonant with its own timeless peace. No ecstasy, only satisfaction. What the hell is my future?

I reached Pen Hill at about three in the afternoon. Gammel had an eye for wide country as well as his own herbaceous border. The rendezvous was well chosen. My small, unidentifiable figure could be seen for miles around and I, too, had a clear view except for woodland at the foot of the steep slope. Obviously that was where I must expect him to show himself.

He did. His appearance was unfamiliar. He was wearing a clerical collar and from the waist up was parson rather than landowner, Christian rather than Anarchist. I hoped this transformation was for the benefit of the police, not to remind the criminal of the incorruptibility of the Church.

Signaling me to follow, he took a path through the woods up the valley of the Churn and turned off into the open, where I lost sight of him in a first fold of the hills. Closing up on where he ought to be I came upon a low, ruined cottage, surrounded by bramble, nettle and fallen stone, and saw him at what remained of a window. The place seemed safe enough for a meeting, offering the temporary cover of interior walls and a deep inglenook in case anyone should pass and give the ruin a casual glance.

He took up a headmasterly position in front of the wide hearth and went straight to the point without any welcome.

"Mr. Johnson, when I invited you to call on me clandestinely I did not think it would cost a man's life."

"In the position that I am in, Sir Frederick, any activity of mine may cost a man's life. I can only ask you to accept that."

"You killed him yourself?"

"Yes. I do not know if your friend in the police has told you what they must have found on his body."

"He has not."

"They will have found a powerful air pistol, some darts and a small phial of poison either to kill or incapacitate."

"I had indeed hoped it was in self-defense. But, sir, the brutality of it!"

"He was already dead when I cut downwards, Sir Frederick. The victims of nuclear fission die more slowly."

"Why did you mutilate him?"

"Anger."

"Anger has no place in war."

126

I should have expected that he would arrive at that parallel for himself, yet it surprised me.

"I know it doesn't," I replied. "But I'd say that most men who have won, say, the Victoria Cross were blazing angry at the time."

"It is generally given for saving the lives of others at the risk of one's own."

"Which involves killing as well as being killed. What exactly were you thinking of when you suggested that an old man is more ready to give his life than a younger?"

"It is true that I foresaw circumstances in which it might be my duty not to escape."

I told him that I foresaw that too, and that meanwhile prevention was better than suicide. Then I drew out the knife and showed it to him.

"Do you know why I carry that, Sir Frederick? Because I will not take life unless I am attacked. I know that my beliefs make that hard to accept. Yet you understood it and told me that I was in hell."

"I did, and now I tell you that hell shall not prevail."

I replied unfeelingly that it did its best most of the time.

"And for the rest of the time what comforts you?"

"My love of this world."

"Are you so sure it's only this one."

"If you mean what I think you mean, Sir Frederick, I don't admit any difference."

"And if *you* mean what I think you mean, dear Julian — here you will let me call you so — you're perfectly right."

He told me about the cottage, saying that in fact it did not belong to anyone. Years ago an old shepherd had died there. According to tradition, locally accepted, he had been given the place as a reward for a long life of service, but there wasn't a document to prove it. The probable owner, whose land adjoined Roke's Tining, considered that the tiny patch of wasteland was not worth the legal expense of establishing his title to it and so it remained as ownerless as a cat gone wild.

"I thought, no doubt romantically, that it could be of use to you," he said. "Meetings? Perhaps for meetings? I take it that you are not working quite alone?"

"Very nearly. One recruit I can trust, and possibly another to come."

"And myself. Of little use I fear, though I can imagine an emergency when you were compromised and I was not. There is also the problem of communication. As you pointed out, we cannot avail ourselves of the club. There was no assistant porter in the box, but I am a pariah. My opinions are too well known. It is hard for many people to believe that I did not know what Shallope was up to. I shall never enter it again. But this cottage — at need you could safely remain here."

The cottage could, as he said, be used for meetings with him or anyone else, though it was uncomfortably close to Roke's Tining, but as a hideout I thought my boardinghouse a lot safer.

"Sixty years ago!" he chuckled. "Sixty years ago when I used to stay with my uncle, the baronet — ah, there are few secrets from little boys! Now you haven't asked me where the shepherd got his water. You thought he walked down to the Churn with a bucket, didn't you?"

I had not thought about water at all. It was one of the most essential points of guerrilla training, but I did not envisage the cottage as Gil's stronghold.

He showed me an open hole in what had been the kitchen floor. Half a dozen steps led down to a little cellar in which was a stone trough fed by a trickle of spring water from a gutter among ferns.

"No more small boys now! The cottage is known to be haunted. Funny to think I naughtily started the rumor myself and now it is accepted mythology. But we'll cover up the cellar all the same."

He drew the remains of a wooden door over the top of the opening.

"Now I feel there is one need of yours more immediate than this," he said. "You're wasting a lot of time in travel and you must badly want a car. It's plain that you can't go around with Herbert Johnson's and you leave a scent behind you if you hire."

He was right on all points. I dared not recover my own car and sell it, and I was reluctant to waste money on buying another when I might want every penny for some unforeseen complication.

He hauled a bundle of notes out of his breast pocket and insisted on my taking it.

"You brought this with you for me?" I asked.

"A golden handshake, Julian, as I believe they call it. I could not hand you over to the police and so very reluctantly I had to assist your escape. I did not expect such very extenuating circumstances. You have a couple of hundred there. It should be enough, paying cash down, for a serviceable secondhand vehicle. Now I shall walk along the hill above this place daily or as frequently as I safely may. How are you to communicate with me if you need me?"

I suggested an arrangement of fallen stones which

could be seen from a distance — two meaning today if possible, three meaning tomorrow.

"And, by the way, Mallant?" he asked.

"Almost certainly, yes."

So we parted on the warmest terms. I had to humor him over his cottage; in fact all future, urgent action is bound to be in London. But I may well consult him. His spirit, as priest or friend, absolves me.

September 1st

I have bought a car with Gammel's money in the name of Herbert Johnson, since logbook and driving license must agree. I don't much like it, but the main point is that my old car and its number were known to my cell, to Rex and to Clotilde, and were — for all I know — on file with the committee. Meetings with Mick are quicker and safer than in a public park.

Elise is established in a top-floor bedroom at a private hotel called Hartwell Lodge. From her window she can see most of the movement in Argyll Square. She watches all day, devotedly carrying out Mick's orders and asking no questions. Mallant maintains his routine.

Mick had a lot of explaining to do after the finding of Vladimir's body had been reported. He was interrogated by Clotilde in her flat — she now seems to have a roving commission directly under the Action Committee — and by a man who by Mick's description must have been Rex. They had no doubt that it was Gil who killed and buried their professional.

Mick thought they had been impressed by his description of the lights and patrols, for they agreed that he was right to clear out before dawn without trying to find the supporting car and that Vladimir had made a grave mistake in not ensuring that he knew its exact position. It appeared that the car should have dropped Vladimir in London and that he should then have reported to Clotilde. Her present flat was as discreet as could be — just a room, kitchen and bath over a garage in a small mews with no other residents.

Helped a little by Mick, they decided that I had waited and waited through the night for a chance to get into Roke's Tining and that Vladimir, too, had waited for me to give away my position. He had attacked when I had abandoned the attempt and was leaving the wood. Rex was careful to repeat to Mick that he wanted me alive, to be certain what game I was playing. Mick thought it possible that he was emphasizing that for the benefit of Clotilde as well. He could not of course ask questions and had to remind himself continually that he knew nothing about the A-bomb and no more than he could have gathered from the press: that some anarchist in Gloucestershire had been manufacturing explosives.

Rex had no doubt that I was actively working against Magma. Clotilde was inclined to believe that I was suffering from nervous strain rather than a traitor. She said angrily that I was a typical professor who wanted facts before acting and was determined to have them. She was quite right about my character but not, I fear, about professors. She had a fascinating theory that battle-happiness — to which she had once referred — had completely overcome me and that I meant to shoot my way in

131

and rescue Gammel. Rex said skeptically that if I was as crazy as that I might just as well have intended to assassinate him.

Clotilde's theory, at first hearing inexplicable, at last gave me the true reason why the committee believed I would try for Roke's Tining and why I had to be stopped. It had nothing to do with Mallant. And it was definite proof that none of them suspected I had talked to both Sir Frederick and Shallope.

Look at it from their point of view! (1) I am an enemy. How far I am an active traitor is uncertain. (2) I take it for granted that Shallope and Gammel willingly manufactured the bomb. The police by this time probably know that Gammel is probably innocent, but I don't and can't know that. (3) Therefore it is Gammel I want to get my hands on in the belief that he will trust me with all he knows or, if he doesn't, I shall be more ruthless than the police in making a dithering old man scream for mercy and talk.

Then Clotilde's and Rex's opposing opinions make sense. Rex knows damned well that I will stick at nothing to get every detail Gammel can tell me. Clotilde, over-influenced perhaps by affection for me, gives me the benefit of the doubt and suggests I was out for a single-handed rescue. It would not in fact have been impossible.

September 3rd

A stroke of luck. Mick paid an early call on Elise to receive her report and to watch Mallant's morning stroll once more for himself. He never appeared, but Rex did.

He showed an interest in a tattered, dusty display of dahlias close to the garden railings. Elise confirmed that Mallant had always done the same. She was sure that there was never anybody else near the dahlias. In the early morning few people were in the garden and she would have noticed any regular visitor.

The answer must be that they are interested in something or somebody on the far side of the square. If that somebody signaled or perhaps was merely in a certain position, then there was no cause for alarm. A fair deduction is that the bomb is nearby. Otherwise I cannot see why Mallant should walk through the square every morning or why Rex should replace him in his absence. If the bomb is somewhere else and it is so important to inspect the site every day, why bother with Argyll Square?

The cache may well be in or under one of the pleasant, shabby Georgian houses. It must be a private house or one converted into flats. To bury or conceal the thing in a small hotel, where movements of staff and guests are incalculable, would be asking for trouble. Argyll Square is a very reasonable choice. Assuming a radius of about two miles for the effect of blast, the explosion flattens the heart of government in Westminster and Whitehall and much of the City and West End. The effect of the uncontrollable firestorm extends out for over three times that area.

This at last gives me some information worth passing to Special Branch. I find I no longer have any objection to calling them in provided I am convinced that their mass intervention has a chance of success. Till now I could be of no use to them. They would certainly be interested in what I could reveal about Magma — which I have no intention of doing — but the subsequent arrests and interrogations would get them no nearer finding the bomb.

In an anonymous note to that Assistant Commissioner Farquhar whom Sir Frederick mentioned I have suggested that Special Branch should examine all drains in and about Argyll Square and check the basements of private houses. To prove the authenticity of the warning, I mentioned that it was an A-bomb of U-235 for which they were searching — a fact still unknown to all but a small circle.

There is a risk that police activity in the right district may convince the Action Committee that the bomb should be exploded before it is too late. I think I am justified in taking the gamble that the police will get to it first, though an uneasy half of me hopes that Argyll Square is after all not the bomb's correct address.

September 4th

The reaction has been immediate and immense, with the army assisting the police. Roads torn up. Sewers exposed. Drains plumbed. In the central garden of Argyll Square bulldozers at work on flowerbeds, lawns and paths. Mine detectors and instruments far more massive than Geiger counters. Everyone in the neighborhood questioned and identities established. Elise had no trouble at all. Like many of our partisans she has never spoken in public, written for the underground press, or openly joined any subversive organization.

They are clever. Streets in Kensington and Paddington

have also been dug up and drains tested so that Argyll Square only appears one of several localities under suspicion.

If the bomb was nothing more than a bluff, what a triumph this disorganization, this chaotic mess would be and how I would have approved and rejoiced! The breakdown of self-satisfied, twopence-off society in those London streets could not be surpassed by flood or fire. Everyone knows that the search is for a large bomb, but not what sort of bomb.

September 5th

Triumph short-lived. Mick tells me that his cell has been ordered out of London and that he has been put in touch — an exceptional move — with the leaders of the other two London cells to arrange dispersal. That means that the Action Committee was prepared to explode the bomb rather than attempt to move it; so the police were dangerously close and my hunch was right. I wonder if the firestorm and fallout will extend as far as Ealing. For myself I don't care if it does. I am helpless.

This morning I was discussing with Mick what to do with Elise. Somebody should be on the spot to continue the watch. Mick insisted that he was going to take her place himself. During the resettlement of local partisans nobody need know that he has not left London. No new group commander had yet contacted him.

He spoke of Elise with an anxiety which for him was unusual and said that I would need her, assuming I got away to any secure future. He doesn't grasp my position

— death, back to jail or for all my life on the run. Of the three I honestly prefer the first. What use am I to a woman or a woman to me?

I replied that if I allowed myself to look forward at all I wanted no sort of tie.

"She'd be disappointed to hear that," he said.

"Romantic fascination, Mick. In normal times I might respond. She's a lovely thing."

"You haven't?"

"No. Why this sudden interest?"

"Friendship."

"She'd be more suited to you."

"To me? Well, she doesn't know it."

It was the slight bitterness in his voice which at last made me understand the full extent of his loyalty.

"Are you that fond of her, Mick?"

"I always have been."

"And no jealousy?"

"Not while I thought you and Clotilde were fixed up. But the last weeks with Elise here and Elise there and me knowing damn well that you were using her but not why — well, jealousy . . . I wouldn't like to call it that, Gil. Sadness, more like. The two people I . . ."

He became incoherent with good North Country embarrassment and we let it go at that. But he couldn't quite bring himself to lay off my supposed affairs of the heart.

"Clotilde, you know. She'd do a lot for you."

"She might have the decency to make it an easy death."

"When I saw her with Rex she believed you were just going your own way and not a serious danger."

"She's got enough evidence."

"Not for her, I reckon. You know what some women are. If you can't do wrong for 'em, then you can't do wrong."

I remember writing something in this diary to the effect that when a man and a woman have worked closely together and meet in new and less businesslike circumstances, curiosity might well lead them to bed. I never thought she could be fulfilling more than curiosity. Yet I do recall that unexpected tenderness. It could be that in all our other transactions she had been proudly withholding herself, duty and discipline being emphasized for her own benefit rather than mine. I had always felt that her command manner was overdone and supposed that she wished to show herself as militant and efficient as any mere male partisan. I was stupid. She was so sure of her quality — and so were the rest of us — that she had no need for that muscular mentality and must have known it.

I asked Mick if he had any really solid reason for his belief.

"Just a dirty mind, Gil. But Elise was very sure. She said Clotilde was never natural with you."

The processes of human intelligence are odd. Sometimes I think the subconscious is a far better planner than the reasoning conscious. At this moment, out of any context, a remark of Sir Frederick came flooding back into memory:

I should not let him go and I should choose for him a London prison.

He underrated Magma. Partisans are expendable and we all know it. But Clotilde? If they thought the Govern-

137

ment had got her, wouldn't they put off the explosion? But the Government would not have her. I would. And then I could count on misunderstandings, bargaining, delay till the position was clarified. If they intended to use the bomb anyway they could very well wait some days in order to get Clotilde back — as was done for her before and now with a far more credible threat.

I told Mick that Elise should remain in her hotel, where she would be safe for a day or two, and that he was to keep in daily touch with me and with her.

Had he noticed a telephone in Clotilde's flat, I asked him. Yes, there was one. That is essential, though I am not yet sure how it is going to be used. Above all it is essential that I leave convincing evidence that the police have arrested her.

God, I am contemplating the very depths of dishonor! But time, time, time — I must have time.

September 6th

I have taken a cautious look at Onslow Mews, a small opening off Onslow Street in Fulham, about fifty yards deep and lined by private garages, one of which, at the bottom end, has been converted to the tiny maisonette which contains Clotilde. It is cleverly selected for her, without inquisitive and inconvenient neighbors, and allows me to devise a plan which in theory will work provided the timing is not too wildly out and there are no unforeseeable accidents. Success also depends on whether the telephone number through which, as group commander, I could reach Rex in the evening is still in use. Mick, being only a cell leader, does not know it.

According to Mick's account of his interview with the pair, Clotilde opposed any drastic measures against me until I was given a chance to explain. It will seem to Rex quite likely that we have been lovers and thus believable that I — in spite of being a traitor and possibly a secret police agent — should warn her through him as soon as I learned that Special Branch or the Anti-Terrorist Squad had found and identified her.

Now I have to work this out on paper. I can only get in touch with Rex at 6:30 in the evening. The dialing code shows that he is then standing by a telephone in Clerkenwell. The number cannot be that of his house or business; otherwise any of the group commanders whom he handles would be able to discover his true name.

Very well. At 6:30 I warn Rex that he should tell Clotilde to get out of her flat and stay out. He is bound to act on that, but he will want to confirm that the police have in fact raided Onslow Mews. He must do that himself, for he has no time to pass orders down to a cell, and anyway they are already dispersed. By taxi or Underground it will take him at least thirty-five minutes to get from Clerkenwell to Fulham.

By that time there will be police cars in the mews and lights on in the flat while it is being thoroughly searched. What Rex, arriving as a casual onlooker, can ask without arousing suspicion is very limited: "What's up, constable?" or "Any luck?" And the police reply will be noncommittal as it always is — more than usually so, considering that the raid is top secret. I can take it that the entrance to the mews will be blocked and therefore — unless someone is trapped inside while garaging his car — there should be no independent witness who can say whether a police car did or did not drive away with a woman.

It's a gamble, a reckless gamble. But the probabilities are that Rex is going to be left in suspense; and when no news at all comes in from Clotilde during the night he must assume that the police have got her.

I'll put through the call to Assistant Commissioner Farquhar immediately after telephoning Rex. Assuming he has given orders that any anonymous communication to him is to be taken seriously — and I'll bet he has — his men will be on the spot and in force within ten minutes, or at any rate well before Rex arrives.

Now for Clotilde. She bolts at once when Rex warns her and Mick picks her up smartly outside the mews. If she is out when Rex calls and returns later she will really be arrested. Another gamble! I have no way of ensuring that she will be in. Neither Mick nor I know her number or the name in which she has rented the flat.

I may improve on my message to Scotland Yard, but something like this, I think, will do:

Urgent for Assistant Commissioner Farquhar, Special Branch. Take it down now because I am not going to hang about for you to trace where this call is coming from. My letter of September third to Farquhar is proof of bona fides. If you raid immediately you will find Miss Alexandra Baratov probably with others at Two Onslow Mews. She was arrested on June twenty-eighth and later released in consequence of a threat of which we both know.

Mick has an estate car. We can hide Clotilde fairly well under blankets and rugs, whereas a woman bound and gagged in an ordinary back seat must be noticed by some

140

passerby. It's a pity that I cannot put her to sleep. When Herbert Johnson vanished into limbo he carried nothing but a suitcase and himself to Ealing. In any case, I never possessed any drugs to be administered orally or by injection; they could be obtained, if judged necessary for any operation, by a group commander from committee stores.

However, I do not think Mick should pick her up in the estate car. A folding bed will be in it, blankets, a Primus stove, a basket of food and drink. All that invites too much curiosity. It will seem more natural if she is rescued in my own car, empty, casual, very ordinary and just right for a short run to safety.

All very tentative. I wonder how I shall look back on this so-called planning.

September 8th

Yesterday evening I left Mick's estate car in a nearby car park and put through my two telephone messages from a box only a minute's walk from Onslow Mews. In speaking to Rex I invented a convincing detail, telling him that his tame assassin had been careless enough to make a note of Clotilde's address and that the police had found it. Myself, I did not know where Clotilde was and could not warn her that her retreat was likely to be raided at any moment if it had not been already. He never questioned my information and tried to keep me talking. I cut him off and got through to Scotland Yard.

Meanwhile Mick had parked my car round two corners from Onslow Street. Five minutes later we were both hanging around on the pavement, with the entrance to the little cobbled mews between us. The long street of four-story brick houses turned into flats was typical of London. There were no shops handy, no pub and nothing in which one could reasonably show an interest, so we could not idle plausibly. Any experienced detective would have spotted us at once. We kept moving back and forth with pedestrians going out for a meal or returning from work. Time passed, and still no Clotilde. A car drove into the mews, and three minutes later a young man came out on foot. He was too short for Clotilde, but Mick and I both converged on him to have a closer look. The ten minutes I had allowed for the police to arrive were nearly up. I dared not enter the mews myself or allow Mick to do so in case we were trapped there and held for questioning.

It was an agony of frustration strolling up and down that damned dead street among damned dead people who would probably be both if I were unable to get hold of Clotilde. I assumed that Rex had smelled a rat. But even if he had he could not take the risk of refusing to telephone her. I wondered if he had laid on some unknown operation with some unknown group commander. But help might not arrive in time and he must know it.

Nearly twenty minutes had gone by when from the direction of the Cromwell Road I heard the siren of a police car tearing through traffic and I began to walk away. Then Mick signaled to me, and at last I saw Clotilde stride very fast out of the mews, look around, and cross the road. She had had no time for any attempt at disguise. She was dressed for the house in blue velvet trousers and a low-cut evening sweater with her fair hair loose on her shoulders — a most obvious Alexandra Baratov, answering to perfection the description of the young woman who had appeared in court and been mysteriously released. Mick closed in on her, and the pair were safely around the corner just before the first car arrived. The duty officer who took down my message must have either been skeptical or had temporary difficulty in contacting anyone of high enough rank to understand its importance.

With Mick and Clotilde safely away I recovered the estate car and set off for the rendezvous. In spite of success, my confidence was shattered. Far too much had depended on luck. Driving out of London I was desperately aware that we had had too little time to plan and none to reconnoiter. The whole pretended rescue seemed amateurish and inefficient. But so it had to be until we reached the ruined cottage which Sir Frederick had shown me.

Clotilde would expect a short journey within London, not a gangster's drive into the country. As soon as her relief had worn off she was bound to see that the operation did not bear the typical Magma hallmarks — quiet, unobtrusive, every move carefully worked out. With this in mind I had plotted a steady route to the northwest which should not give her any impression of panic or of a search for solitude since it ran from string to string of suburban towns and villages and took suddenly to wilder country where she could be quickly overpowered. Chesham, I remembered, about filled the bill. On the way there Mick was to say that he had been ordered — but how? — to take her straight to the committee and that she would change cars outside Chesham. It was possible. Both she and I accepted that the committee might meet anywhere but did not expect to know all the possible places. In present circumstances, a house at a safe distance from London would appear very natural.

Our rendezvous was to be in Pednor Bottom, a lane running from Chesham up one of the remoter Chiltern valleys. I had arranged with Mick that he was to drive slowly so that I could get there before him and choose a safe spot. There were no turnings and he could not miss me. But from that point on we should have to play it by ear.

I drove along Pednor Bottom soon after eight in the falling dusk. The long, straight lane was much as it appeared on the map. On the crests, both sides of the narrow valley, lights twinkled from houses rather too close for comfort. There was hardly any traffic, but enough to impress upon me that whatever we did would have to be done fast. A belt of trees on the left of the road promised to be useful if we had to hide a helpless Clotilde in a hurry. I parked in a gateway on the right where I was partly off the road, yet Mick could see me clearly as he approached.

He arrived ten minutes later and pulled up under the trees well behind me, wisely leaving the engine running. I walked back to the car and opened the door for Clotilde. She got out with a little exclamation of surprise, apparently pleased.

"You ran that close, Clotilde," I said. "You must have been glad to see Mick."

"Yes. I was drying my hair and I let the telephone ring," she replied calmly.

I did not question this. I was too fascinated by the fact that history could be affected by a woman refusing to answer the telephone because she was drying her hair. How well Clotilde knew me!

"Lucky that Rex tried again!"

"And then he had no time to say anything but 'Run!'"

I was satisfied and relieved that as yet there was no need for violence. We could carry on with our plan of continuing with both cars so that Mick could return in his own and mine left somewhere safe, not too far from the cottage.

"I'll drive with Gil now," she said. "God, I'm such a mess!"

She began to walk towards the estate car, then stopped in the beam of Mick's headlights, drew a compact from her handbag, and looked in the mirror. She put back the compact and her hand returned with a .32 automatic. My position was hopeless — not near enough for attack, not far enough away for her to miss. She made me clasp my hands behind my head and ordered me to walk across the road to the edge of the deep ditch on that side.

This was death and I knew it. She had had her orders, was convinced by the evidence, and would obey. I felt that one way or another I deserved what was coming to me and tried — this is true and I am amazed at it — to concentrate on some great pleasure that I could carry with me if there was any I.

I heard Mick start like a banger and was kissed by the breath of the bullet just under my ear. She turned, fired again, and shattered the windscreen, but missed Mick.

145

Then he was on her as she jumped sideways and ran for the shelter of the estate car. He swerved and the right wing caught her and flung her into the hedge. He slued back across the lane in an almost impossible effort to miss the estate car, but he did miss it and finished up with my car on its side and the hood stove in against a tree.

Two distant headlights were approaching from Chesham. We picked up Clotilde and her gun, laid her in the back of the estate car, and were away before the on-coming driver could catch sight of our number. I sat in the back, holding her steady. She was unconscious. Her mouth and cheek were bleeding. Her right shoulder had taken a battering and was scored by the hawthorn, but her arm did not seem to be broken.

"Why the devil didn't she hold up both of us while she could?" I asked.

"I persuaded her that I was sent by you. I've never been told that you are no longer my group commander," Mick explained. "I know you are under some kind of cloud, but that's all."

"She didn't show any suspicion?"

"No. A bit of luck for us, I thought. It looked as if we could drive over half England with her saying thank you very much."

I saw now that she had talked to Rex till the very last moment — a long conversation in which he had said, in effect, I told you so, and ordered her to do a better job than Vladimir. I was a fool to have embroidered my conversation with Rex with that bit about Clotilde's address being found on Vladimir's body. It was proof positive that I was in communication with the police.

It was a vile order to have given her, but I suppose she was able to take refuge in that military restraint which she had shown in all her earlier dealings with her favorite cell leader. One must remember, too, that she was fanatically proud and that I had been grossly unfaithful to her trust in me.

As soon as we were clear of the Chilterns, Mick stopped and I arranged the seat cushions to make her as comfortable as I could while Mick boiled a kettle for hot tea. She came around and her color improved. She was in no condition to move or yell, but it now seemed that she was out of danger from serious shock.

An hour and a half later we were beneath Pen Hill and on a passable track with plenty of cover on both sides. In the darkness it took me some time to find the right route through the trees to the open, and even then it was hard to pick up the irregular outline of the ruin. That cottage had existence without presence.

After transporting the stores, we carried Clotilde on the folding bed and took her down the steps to the well cellar. Cold and damp it was below ground on a September night, but at least we could safely show a light. When Mick left, we arranged that he should park the car at any handy village lower down the valley and come back on foot early in the afternoon, which would give me time to get in touch with the reverend baronet and to go to work on Clotilde.

She slept uneasily till dawn. Now that the bruises had come up she was a shocking sight, one side of her face swollen, striped by shallow scratches and with a round, blue lump. She could not move her right arm without considerable pain. She told me that a tooth had been knocked out and that she thought her collarbone was broken. I fed her hot soup, for she could not take any solid food. We spoke with reserve but quite amicably, as if we were two strangers.

I left her alone while I set up the two stones to alert Sir Frederick, meanwhile putting back the heavy door over the cellar entrance. She was indomitable. When I returned I found her collapsed at the foot of the steps. She had tried to lift the door and escape.

"You might just as well let me go, Gil," she said. "I don't know where the bomb is, so it's no good twisting my arm."

I could have told her myself that it was no use. If she did know she would never confess it whatever agony I caused her and instead would invent a convincing hiding place with a detailed description. Torture to my mind is a futile method of arriving at truth unless the interrogator is already in a position to know which gasping confession cannot possibly be fact; and if he knows that much he should not need torture at all. I can imagine it might occasionally be of value when the victim has no code of honor and nothing to lose but freedom from pain.

"I have quite a different reason for rescuing you, Clotilde," I said. "You mustn't believe all Rex tells you."

I could see she was intrigued by this. There was a chance that if I kept interrogation on an even, friendly keel I might get a clue to what limited knowledge she had. She could not guess that my real intention in kidnapping her was merely to persuade Magma to delay the explosion while they forced the Government, as they supposed, to release her.

"But you knew that the police had found out my address and were on their way."

"I did."

"How?"

"Some of the committee have their own informants."

"And the police have theirs," she retorted.

"No. No, I don't think so," I answered peaceably.

"Then what else are you?"

"Rex should not have hired Vladimir to kill me. For some of us that was the last straw."

"You cannot use me to split Magma!"

So that was in her mind! She was half ready to accept that I might not be a police agent but an ambitious group commander who hoped to profit by the explosion rather than to prevent it. I had only been sparring for an opening, searching for the point where hatred of me ended and old friendship began. I decided to go along with her tentative theory, which gave us something to talk about.

"Do I have to be as ruthless as you and lock you up in London?"

"We should arrive too late, my dear Gil."

That was the first useful piece of information. I had assumed that the cells had been evacuated because the police were on a hot scent at Argyll Square. It was worse than that. The chosen date was now, or nearly now.

"If we do, the mass grave will come in handy."

She spotted that as a slice of unnecessary horror film and did not reply, asking casually:

149

"Where are we?"

"The Bomblayers Arms, let us say."

"Boy Scout camp?"

"You forget, Clotilde, that I am still a group commander."

"You are not!"

"You think Mick is the only one who accepts me? I always told you that we overdid security. The committee has a problem of communication, especially now."

"Gil, you're a fool! A dreamer like you could never lead. It isn't in you."

There's some truth in that, I admit, in the sense that I would never make a chief of staff. But I can lead partisans and I know it.

"Not even a minor Trotsky to a Lenin?"

"Where's your Lenin?"

"You don't know the International Committee. I do. What about Mallant?"

"Who is he?"

Her tone was so contemptuous that it was certain she had never heard of him under his own name. I described for her his eyes and his beard and could tell from her silence that she had at least met him and was giving nothing away.

"You will know after the explosion."

"You don't mean to interfere then?"

"Certainly not. I know where the bomb is. Rex kept me out of the move from Hoxton, but I was connected with Argyll Square."

"God! William the Builder!" she exclaimed.

Her surprise was genuine. It was plain that she did not know the site of the bomb, but now realized that if it was in or near Argyll Square this William the Builder had played some essential part.

I said that he was a natural choice and asked what his real name was. She replied that only the committee knew that, which may or may not have been true.

So I let our talk go at that. Clotilde had not denied that I might be better informed than she was, and I did not want to spoil the impression by asking more questions.

I wish I knew more of Rex and could have used him as a lever to force more indiscretions out of her. The man is only a ghost who told me at great length of an inferno to come. A ghost he remains and has to remain, for I cannot waste precious time in trying to discover his true identity. I think he is head of the British Action Committee and responsible for our exaggerated security — in his own interest as well as Magma's. If ever I can loose Special Branch on the bomb or deal with it myself, the police can deal with Rex afterwards. At least I can tell them that he works or occasionally works for the newspaper office where Alexandra Baratov disappeared after she was released from arrest.

I shut her down in the cellar again, advising her to have patience until my party was successful, when I would decide what to do with her.

"A woman who is prepared to execute an old friend without a qualm can be useful to us," I added.

The unexpected clue of William the Builder could be vital. However, speculation got me nowhere and still does. Our transport at Blackmoor Gate belonged or purported to belong to a builder. The name on it was Groads Construction Company, certainly false and easily changeable. It's a fair bet that William was also responsible for the moves from Roke's Tining to Hoxton and from Hoxton to the final site. So why Clotilde's surprise? Who but a builder could convincingly dig up and prepare — perhaps some months ago — the underground nest for the bomb?

During the morning I sat behind what was left of a first-floor wall, from which I could see the edge of the hills above the cottage and the strip of woodland, whispering with the flight of birds, along the Churn below. Nobody passed but a good woman with a basket looking for the first blackberries. She did not come up as far as the cottage, though there were already black beads among the crimson clusters on the surrounding brambles. Evidently young Frederick's ghost story had passed down the years intact.

He turned up himself at midday with the news that the group of police and scientists had at last left Roke's Tining. No charge had been made against him, but he had been requested not to reopen his colony for the present. In case his trust in me was shaken — a week's absence can make a big difference — I told him at once that I had written anonymously to his Assistant Commissioner Farquhar informing him with convincing details where I suspected the bomb was hidden. Police and army had then turned streets and drains inside out with no success.

Gammel replied that he had heard of the search from the now friendly superintendent. His bosses had been sure that their informant was reliable and were completely beaten. They had even consulted a clairvoyant who on occasions had given them a lead, or rather — so the skeptical superintendent had said — a chance to pack up their preconceived ideas and use some imagination.

152

The clairvoyant produced a whole rigmarole of nonsense which fitted neither drains nor Argyll Square, but insisted on the importance of "flying" or "fly." If the bomb was to be dropped on London, they could do little about it beyond tightening up the air traffic controls.

With that out of the way, I put Sir Frederick in the picture, explaining that I had grabbed one of Magma's most valuable leaders and left evidence that she had been arrested. To my mind it was certain that they would delay the explosion in order to use the threat of it to get her back. Meanwhile they had no reason to fear discovery.

"The poor woman is down below?" he asked.

This unexpected pity had to be diverted. I gave him some account of what had happened and how she had tried to execute me.

"She will be badly hurt. I must have a look at her, Julian. I am not without experience."

Foolishly, I saw no reason why he should not. My attitude towards Clotilde was coldly utilitarian. I had not yet decided how or where I intended to return her, if at all, but she could be of no use to me desperately ill or dead.

I took him down to the well cellar, replaced the hatch, and lit a lamp. As well as the scarred and swollen face, Clotilde's hair and clothes were matted with blood. Sir Frederick took off into the nineteenth century.

"Will you allow me to examine you, dear lady? I am, I assure you, a Clerk in Holy Orders, though for the moment not habited as such."

He formally sent me upstairs. I was not unsympathetic, but Clotilde was Clotilde. I quietly showed her that the .32 was in my pocket.

153

Gammel came up very worried, telling me that the collarbone was broken, that she had lost a molar, and that he suspected a fracture of the jaw.

"She cannot remain here in the cold," he said.

"She has to."

"Julian, I will not permit you to treat a woman in that way whatever she has done."

"Sex discrimination, Sir Frederick?"

"Very well, sir! You find chivalry outdated. But Christianity remains. If I can help the suffering, I must do so."

I saw that I was up against the romantic ideals of both the baronet and the priest — a powerful combination. But I flatly refused to let her go.

"I am not demanding that you let her go. I require that she be put in my care, be warmed, fed, and healed so far as is in my power. From the little you have said I gather that you vaguely perceive a duty towards God, but you are too self-centered to be aware of duty to the neighbor."

I asked him angrily what the hell else I was doing.

"Yes, you are prepared to sacrifice yourself, but now as formerly you have little pity for the individual. Whether you wish it or not, I shall take this unfortunate girl into my house."

I was dependent on him and could see no way out. Roke's Tining was empty. The policewomen who had attended to domestic chores had gone, and neither colonists nor staff had returned. I protested that even a Good Samaritan might draw the line at a wounded lioness.

"He might well, Julian. On the other hand, Androcles

did not. So I shall conform to the pagan parable while of course agreeing that you should provide a guard."

He had still not realized how alone I was, presuming that I could lay my hands on some devoted remnant of partisans. I had only Mick. Not much for the fantastic Trotsky figure which had given Clotilde something to think about! And Mick I could not spare. Elise then? Her former medical studies must be quite enough to deal with bruises and minor fractures.

I told Sir Frederick that he could have Clotilde at Roke's Tining. He was to prepare a secure room and come back at dusk. We could only dare to shift Clotilde after dark.

Mick when he arrived in the afternoon was of course overjoyed at the prospect of getting Elise out of London. To keep her on in her hotel room must have been a severe test of his loyalty — to me or to conscience or to what? He believed that she would not question my orders and that it was unnecessary to tell her all the truth till we were very sure that she would not consider the corpses of London a just revenge for the corpses of Africa. Meanwhile explanation was easy; we had only to swap the facts around. Clotilde was suspected of disloyalty. I had been ordered to detain her. Elise knew of Clotilde's secret negotiations with Shallope. She knew of Shallope's assassination. We had merely to say that Clotilde had no right to take a line of her own.

I determined to return to London myself, leaving Mick in charge of Clotilde and — perhaps the harder task — Sir Frederick. The risk of showing myself in Argyll Square was considerable but had to be taken. William the

Builder was haunting me and could not be ignored. On the spot I might discover or learn through casual questions how and where he had delivered his load.

So here I am back at my Ealing boardinghouse. The transfer of Clotilde from cellar to house was without incident, and all should be well until I can return with Elise and release Mick. He and Sir Frederick were soon on easy terms, each recognizing the essential simplicity of the other. What nonsense! To my way of thinking, both of them are highly complicated characters. Yet I shouldn't wonder if that impulsive bit of insight is right.

September 9th

It has worked. The Action Committee has ordered the Government to release Clotilde immediately. They have come out of the shadows and used the name of Magma, never publicized till now, without any attempt to divert attention to the Irish, Palestinians or Trotskyists. A copy of the ultimatum has apparently gone to all the principal morning papers with a demand that the Government's reply also be transmitted through the press. What arrogance and authority!

NOTICE TO THE GOVERNMENT
Miss Alexandra Baratov, now again in police custody, will be immediately released. If you refuse, the campaign of destruction of which you have already been warned will be carried out. You will reply by public announcement in the press that you accept.

We will then instruct you privately how and when to release her.

The ultimatum still does not state the nature of the destruction. Evidently Magma is reluctant as yet to provoke the terror and the mass exodus. The committee has, I think, still another objective: to ensure that the prevarications of the Cabinet and all the lies of mistaken identity at the time of Clotilde's real arrest five weeks ago will be remembered, thus inflaming the hatred and contempt of those citizens left alive.

It's a bold and ingenious idea to publicize the threat, and so avoid any clue to the organization and leaders of Magma. Since we insist on a public reply, the demand must also be printed, though I doubt it would be if editors-in-chief were not in on the secret of the bomb and in hourly touch with the authorities.

I wonder what on earth the Cabinet will reply. My guess has always been that they will crawl and whine and swear quite truthfully that they have not got Clotilde. Neither Magma nor the public will believe it, but for three or more days of negotiation London is reprieved. I, I alone, have done this. Triumph is overwhelmed by the futility of it. How am I to profit by my gain of days? I am like a man who has put off his execution and wonders why he bothered.

But let me use the gain, such as it is, and continue with my routine of recording events in case a chink of light shows through the prison wall. William the Builder?

This morning I cautiously made my way to Elise's hotel

after the hour when I knew Mallant — or Rex standing in for him — would have passed. It was pretty certain that Magma would have followed our usual practice — I still cannot help this "our" — of not putting out observers who are as likely to attract the attention of police as to give warning against them. To post partisans in and around Argyll Square would be particularly dangerous. All the same, I did my best not to conform to the probable description of me. I dressed in Herbert Johnson's most imposing suit, carried a briefcase, and wore a hat, which normally I never do.

Elise, following her orders exactly, was in her room. She had had some trouble in explaining why she never left it except for meals, letting it be known that she was writing an urgent report on the Saharan disasters. She had backed her story by leaving sheets of manuscript around together with a collection of books on malnutrition and tropical diseases. Dutifully she did not press me for any explanation, assuming that Magma was planning some stroke of sabotage more daring than usual and needed to know all movements on the ground.

She had nothing to report except the continual activity of plainclothes detectives. The identities of everyone in the hotel and presumably in all other hotels had been checked. Two of the kitchen staff had been taken away for questioning — one a Portuguese believed to be a Communist, the other a Chinaman without an immigration permit. Some of the more nervous guests had left after the formidable search of the drains. The less imaginative were of the opinion that if there had ever been a bomb the police and army would have discovered it, so they were safer where they were than anywhere else. She had cultivated the proprietress of the hotel, a talkative lady as well informed about the doings of the neighborhood as any village postmistress, in fact the perfect minor agent. All the questions asked by the police of landladies and householders and all scares and suspicions which had sent them rushing to the telephones had been passed on to Elise. There had been near panic when some dear old lady — or Magma? — had flooded the district with a rumor that any pulling of plugs or running of water might set off a bomb.

It was pointless to ask her if she had noticed any stationary builder's trucks, for she had arrived after the bomb was in position and there was no reason why Groads Construction Company should have returned. When I asked her to find out if any private houses or hotels had recently been converted or rebuilt, she replied that the police had not overlooked that point and had checked all recent repairs, paying particular attention to porticos, basements and even chimney stacks as well as drains.

Her response to the threat in the morning papers was one of pride and triumph, making it impossible for me to carry out the plan of persuading her that Clotilde was a traitor. Not at all! We had been ordered to rescue her, had done so, and were keeping her safe in the country.

Elise was dewy-eyed — the pretty thing — over the glorious martyr, Clotilde, and her gallant group commander. GGC was in no mood to respond and told her what a wonderful chap Mick was, lonely, loving and of

superb courage. Quite apart from seeing that Mick got
his deserts, I felt that the closer they were the more I
could trust them to work in harmony.

I described Clotilde's injuries and told Elise to pack
whatever she was likely to need for provisional treatment
and the relief of pain. She was to take her own car — a
second would be useful — stop at Andoversford and
telephone Sir Frederick Gammel, saying that she had
been sent by Gil's Agency to apply for the post of housekeeper but was unable to find Roke's Tining. That would
sound reasonable and innocent if the telephone were
tapped and would bring out Mick, who would decide
what to do with her car.

I myself stayed on in London, still with the wild hope of
seeing, hearing or feeling in my bones something that
Special Branch had missed. I had a long look across the
rubble of Argyll Square where the dahlias had been. The
most likely spot where, by watching for a face or a signal,
Mallant could have assured himself that the weapon was
in order and undiscovered appeared to be a house on the
opposite side of the square numbered 71, which was divided into small flats. That had also occurred to Elise,
who led her useful proprietress to talk about the tenants
— with no positive result beyond the assurance that the
police had mercilessly put them all through the laundry.

But it was too dangerous to hang about or pass down
any street more than once. As Elise had said, the district
crawled with plainclothes police, two of whom, fairly obvious to a practiced eye, got into conversation with me in
the saloon bars of pubs. So in the dusk I returned to

Ealing, glad to be in my temporary home with time to think, though I only go around and around in circles.

September 10th

Just a breakfasttime note on the news before I leave for Roke's Tining. The Cabinet has shown some intelligence and replied, publicly as demanded, that Alexandra Baratov is being held under the Terrorist Act, that this country and its freely elected Government do not surrender to blackmail, and that the Law will follow its normal course.

Cunning rather than desperate courage, I think. They decided that if they denied any knowledge of Clotilde no basis for negotiations would be left, but by stating that they have got her they hope — much as I did — to gain a few days. In fact they have been more successful than they can imagine. I doubt if Government or police has any exact picture of the long-term objectives and ruthlessness of Magma, or dreams that if it were not for the committee's resolve to save Clotilde from incineration the bomb would have gone off already and will go off as soon as they have her back.

I also suspect that Special Branch, whose chiefs must have been present at that agonizing Cabinet meeting, had reason to be more confident. Have they got a new lead? I hope to God they have.

But I have made a bad mistake as a result of this unexpected move. Elise will see a morning paper. How can

Mick explain my story that we had rescued Clotilde? And what is Elise going to say in conversation with her?

September 10th — midnight

Holed up and defiant. Let these urban guerrillas catch me if they can! The police are now far more dangerous since Julian Despard has come to life for them. By now they must have matched his fingerprints and know that he is Herbert Johnson. I wish they could also know that he is the one person with a faint hope of preventing the holocaust.

Prove it, they would demand; but I cannot. The only proof is the bomb itself. Rex's identity is unknown to me, Mallant's involvement without a scrap of evidence. In a matter of weeks or months, starting from what I can tell them, they might be able to penetrate Magma and smash it. But they have not got weeks or months. Hours? It could be hours.

I should have foreseen it. I should have burned that wrecked car. There it was, crying aloud for investigation of the bullethole in the windscreen and Clotilde's blood in the ditch alongside. But I had no time. As it was, Mick and I were lucky to get clear just before the oncoming headlights were near enough to read the number of the estate car.

That secondhand car of mine was registered in the name of Herbert Johnson with a false address. A common name. In the normal way it would have taken some leisurely passing of files before the police traced the identity of the owner. But they are fighting for life — their own as well as that of the city — and God knows how many memory banks are ticking away to the tune of Roke's Tining. A few seconds of computer time would be enough to show that a Herbert Johnson, publisher's representative, called on Sir Frederick Gammel with a hired car and a not very satisfactory story of what had happened to his own. And the fingerprints on that wreck in Pednor Bottom? One collective yell of triumph from Special Branch! They are Julian Despard's.

This morning I drove back into the Cotswolds determined to extract from Clotilde whatever William the Builder meant to her. Having parked the estate car in Chedworth as usual, I walked to the cottage to wait for Mick, whom I had instructed to call there every day at about two o'clock in case I had returned with news. It was far too risky to telephone my movements.

When he turned up he was worried and depressed. The police had been at Roke's Tining the previous afternoon for a further search of the spot where Vladimir had been killed and the leaves where he had been buried. When Elise telephoned he thought it best to tell her to stay at Andoversford for the night and come out in the morning.

On her arrival she told him that she had read the Government's reply to the ultimatum. Mick was in a quandary and took refuge in silence, always effective with Elise, who never committed the security sin of asking questions. He guessed that when I had ordered her out to Roke's Tining I might have dropped the story of Clotilde's treachery and accounted for her presence by the simpler, more convincing explanation that we had rescued her. But now that would hardly do. He had decided to let the matter ride until she had talked to Clotilde and he knew what line of defense he must take.

Elise went in at once to Clotilde, fired him out of the room during her examination — he should have refused to go, but one must forgive the doglike obedience of the lover — and remained half an hour. He did listen at the door, but it was of sturdy oak five hundred years old and the bed was far away from it, so he heard nothing but a cry of horror. When Elise came out, her face was pale and set and her eyes blazing. She refused to speak to him, saying that she would carry out her medical duties and nothing more.

I asked what she had said to Sir Frederick.

"Stonily polite she was. Treated him as if he was a screw in a jail for high-class tarts. Poor old Fred is suffering from conscience. He doesn't believe in knocking 'em about."

"He doesn't think we knocked Clotilde about, does he?"

"Put it this way, Gil! He thinks we should have taken care she wasn't knocked about, thinks we should have said: 'Please, madam, be good enough to step out of the way of the car and point that gun t'other way.' "

When I arrived at the house I got the same treatment from Elise. No more dewy eyes. For all she knew I was still her group commander, so I was stern. She responded with equal sternness, omitting any report of what had upset her as if I must know it already.

I went up at once to see Clotilde. Gammel had chosen her room intelligently. It was on the third floor with a window looking only on to the courtyard. No tempting ledge or drainpipe was near it and she could not escape — being unable to knot sheets with one hand — without a shattering drop to the cobbles below. There was a wash-basin in the room with an old-fashioned geyser for hot water and she had been provided with an antique mahogany commode for her needs.

She looked better than when we had moved her from the cottage and, as I recognized from the lowered lids, in the mood for attack. It was difficult to restart interrogation on new lines because I had already claimed to know where the bomb was concealed. She herself had not been in on the secret, but my mention of Argyll Square had revealed to her a possible hiding place and the man who had constructed it.

I began to talk around the transport from Roke's Tining to Hoxton and Hoxton to the prepared site, but got nothing out of her except that William the Builder was a cell leader.

"He made a good job of the cache," I said.

"Of the garden railings? Yes. He left the hole underground when he repaired them a year ago."

"Try again, Clotilde! The police would have found it."

"Who sent them to Argyll Square, Gil? Rex could think of no one but you."

"If I meant them to find it, I should have sent them to the right spot."

"But you couldn't because all you know is that it is in a drainpipe. You were quite convincing, my minor Trotsky, but you shouldn't let prisoners lie in a comfortable bed with time to think."

What she had had was not time to think, but the news in the morning papers. I tried the line of swearing I had rescued her because I could not contemplate the long sentence she would get.

"Long sentence? They can prove nothing. You hoped to screw information out of me which the police never could. But it won't help you, Gil, and I will tell you lie after lie to avoid more torture."

"Torture?"

"Elise considers my tooth was knocked out by a blunt instrument. A round mallet, say."

"If she can't tell the difference between a swipe from a car and a block of wood . . ."

"The car hit my shoulder. If it had hit my face it would have broken cheek and jaw, not just knocked out a molar. Look at the round bruise!"

"Evidence insufficient. You must have fallen on the stump of a sapling or something."

"Oh, there is more evidence, Gil. You ask little Elise!"

So she had convinced Elise that I was not only a traitor to Magma but a determined and brutal interrogator. By God, she made me think seriously of torture! Useless, of course. She would, as she said, have told me lie after lie till I was sick of it.

I went out to deal with Elise, meaning to be gentle, for it was not her fault that she had been deceived. The only certainty the poor girl had was that the Government held

Clotilde and that it stood to reason I must be a Government agent.

I found her in the garden, flitting up and down with her fists clenched, and asked her whether she believed it likely, from all she knew of us, that Mick and I were working for the police.

"Mick, no!" she replied bitterly. "I think he is your stooge like I am. And you — I accept your orders because I don't know any better, but that doesn't mean I don't wonder about them. Who is using me? The police, the committee or you for some game of your own?"

"What did Clotilde tell you I wanted from her?"

"To know where the new arms depot is."

"What sort of arms?"

"I suppose those we landed at Blackmoor Gate."

"And when she wouldn't tell me?"

"You tortured her. You cannot deny it."

"She was knocked down by a car when trying to kill me and hit her cheek on a stump in the hedgerow."

"And hit her pubic hair on a stump too?"

I told her to come with me at once to Clotilde's room. She was ready for us, hunched on her side and turning only her head with now open and innocent eyes.

"Not again, Gil! Not again!" she moaned.

I was brutal and foolish. I threw off the bedclothes and ripped off the dressing. Elise tried to prevent me but Clotilde cleverly put up no fight at all. She had deliberately burned those rare golden curls with a match and then pressed on the bare skin in two places a coin — or something round — heated on the element under the geyser. I do not know whether a doctor or torturer would have been deceived, but to Elise it was obvious that two electrodes had been attached to her private parts. Nobody but Clotilde could have thought it up and endured the pain.

It had been done of course before the arrival of Elise and was not meant for her at all. It was for Sir Frederick's benefit — if the Clerk in Holy Orders could be persuaded to have a good look. And it would have worked. He would have secretly set her free while Mick and I suspected nothing and never spoken to us again. She had summed him up to perfection.

As for her choice of such a delicate and traditional spot to be tortured, I feel there was in it an element of personal revenge as well as a symbolic destruction of her former affection for the rat Gil. It is so often from such trivialities, like the stumble of a skier which starts an avalanche, that disaster broadens and thunders on to us.

In the late afternoon Ian Roberts telephoned Sir Frederick from Gloucester to say that the police had just left his shop after questioning him about the movements and character of Herbert Johnson, whom they had certainly muddled up with some badly wanted criminal using the same name. They were on their way to Roke's Tining to interview Sir Frederick. He was not to be alarmed. Johnson was well known and above suspicion.

The hell he was! Mr. Johnson was at Roke's Tining while Shallope and his bomb were still in residence. He called again when it had just been removed. And Mr. Johnson's prints were those of Julian Despard, anarchist and jailbreaker.

Myself, I could disappear, but all that was damning evidence against my dear baronet. There could be still worse. If his study had been bugged and if the tapes were rerun now that fresh suspicion had been aroused, they were likely to show the possible movement of a second person on the very night when Vladimir was brutally murdered.

Sir Frederick begged me to run for the cottage at once.

"I shall swear that I have never set eyes on you since the afternoon when you called with Roberts's message of sympathy. I regret that I must tell a lie, but it is a moral imperative."

I told him that he would have to talk in the end. As it was, it had taken him a fortnight to persuade Special Branch of his innocence and he would never be able to do it again.

"And with Clotilde under your roof, nobody will believe you."

"What are you going to do with her?"

"Leave her. In half an hour she will be getting proper treatment in a hospital under guard."

"Then I shall come with you and share with you," he answered. "It is not only to the police that I have to prove I am not guilty."

"Who else?"

"Myself."

If he had insisted on staying I should have had to remove Clotilde to save him, but if the house were emptied I could leave her. Let the police find her and take her away! We were no worse off, and our parliamentary rulers would be amazed to discover that for once they had told the truth.

Hurriedly we consulted Mick. It was essential that he, too, should clear out at once. Nothing was known against him by the police and nothing by Magma as long as Clotilde was out of circulation.

He reminded me that Elise's car was in the courtyard — very naturally, since she had applied for the job of housekeeper — and that we could all escape in it provided we started immediately and had the luck not to meet the police arriving. But Elise herself was another problem. I was sure that in her present mood she would not desert Clotilde. She had a good chance of being able to brazen it out by swearing she had come for a job and found herself nursing a mysterious, tortured woman. Clotilde would back her story.

"You mustn't leave her," Mick insisted. "She's in the clear as I am. You may need both of us and I can manage her. Once in London I know a place for you."

"Shall I pack?" Sir Frederick asked.

"For a night or two. Quickly!"

"But we may be away for weeks. On the run, I believe you call it."

"You'll be in the area of maximum devastation, Fred," Mick said. "One way or the other you won't need clothes for long."

We ran upstairs to Elise's room and told her that we had to move out fast. Explanations later.

"Who will look after Clotilde?" she asked.

"Sir Frederick."

Gammel spoiled that one by trotting up to join us, bag in hand.

"But he is going too."

I was just about to grab Elise and bundle her downstairs and into the car by force when Mick spotted my intention.

"Why not take Clotilde back to the cottage?" he suggested.

I saw what he was after. He didn't want to share the blame for violence on his Elise and, as he had pointed out, both of us might need her if we could recover her good will. So I hesitated, wondering whether the cottage was a possible alternative.

Deadly indecision lasted just long enough for Elise to dash up to the third floor. Seconds later she was back again assisting Clotilde, still in her bloodstained sweater and velvet trousers. It was an intolerable position — one reverend and too chivalrous baronet, one foolish girl determined to save Clotilde from more torture by me and arrest by the police, and Mick with an impulsive plan which couldn't work. It had been essential all along that Clotilde be left in her bedroom unsuspecting.

The car was in the courtyard. Elise turned it to face the arched entrance and left the engine running. I said that Mick was to sit beside her because he knew the way.

"Where are you taking me?" Clotilde asked.

"Back to the cottage. You'll have to walk a little way from the track."

The only plan I could think of was that Mick and I should go up, shut her down in the cellar, and tell the other two we would be back for her later. The chances were that we never would go back and she would die before she was found, but there was nothing else for it.

We helped Clotilde into the back. Then, with three doors open and the three of us about to get in, Elise made the only clear-cut decision of the preceding ten minutes. She was off with a racing start, leaving me sprawled on the cobbles and Mick hanging on to the nearside door until he was in danger of being scraped off by the wall of the arch.

Could I have suspected it? Not then, but now I see Elise's motive. My mention of the cottage did it. She knew nothing about the cottage except that it was some sinister ruin where I had tortured Clotilde. She guessed that we had considered leaving Clotilde, who, no doubt, had whispered: "Help me to escape!" The rest Mick and I had done, without time, without plan, and forced by the idiosyncrasies of our companions into a muddle.

They had gone straight up the valley lane to the Gloucester road. I said they were bound to run into the cops.

"So what?" Mick replied. "Elise is unknown and the Gloucester police aren't looking for Clotilde. They won't be stopped if Elise lends her a coat. Just Brunhilda and her girlfriend doing a tour of the Cotswolds!"

I could only pray that he would be proved wrong. If Clotilde reached Rex and Rex reached Mallant, she would tell them that Gil knew too much and that any more delay was dangerous.

We decided that it was pointless to take refuge in the cottage and that our best chance was to reach the estate

172

car on foot; so we followed the stream down the valley, concentrating on avoiding any human eyes rather than speed and led by Gammel who knew every house, contour and footpath. We had covered less than a mile when two police cars, weaving fast up the road to Roke's Tining, shattered the green quiet of the evening.

That was the route we should have followed if we had got away in Elise's car, taking it for granted that the police would start from Gloucester. In fact Special Branch must have been on their way to us from London while the local police were interviewing Ian Roberts. Elise and Clotilde, against all the odds, were clear away.

Chance evens out. After our bad luck, incompetence or both, the rest was mercifully smooth. Mick and I retrieved his car from Chedworth, picked up Sir Frederick from the cover where we had hidden him, and tucked him up on the floor. He was the wanted man and a conspicuous, unmistakable figure — though, thank God, not clerically dressed — whereas we two were not expected. The police would find immediate evidence that Gammel and two women had departed very suddenly, but only more exhaustive investigation could reveal the presence of two other men.

I thought it unlikely that they would be on to my Ealing hideout as yet. It would take a day or two to connect the transient occupier of that shabby room with Herbert Johnson. When we reached London, Mick called at the house for me and detected no interest or suspicion, so I returned to collect my bag with this diary and other minor possessions — the bill had been paid in advance — and we were away again.

Away, yes. But still only half an hour ahead of disaster. The final edition of the evening papers carried a description of the terrorist Herbert Johnson. It was not very flattering, dramatically speaking of a lurching gait (springy would have been the right word, Mick assured me) and the piercing blue eyes of a killer. They had a meaningless Photofit picture of my present face but no photograph. I had always been careful that none should exist.

Before we left Roke's Tining Mick had mentioned that he knew of a possible place for us. He now went off to inspect it while Gammel and I wandered about separately, arranging to meet him on the dark towpath near Kew Bridge. When he returned to collect us he said that all was in order and that he had the right clothes for us together with two bedrolls which would be our only furniture.

We changed quickly under the trees. For Sir Frederick there was a foul suit of worn tweeds. One could swear that he was spending his old-age pension on methylated spirits and sleeping rough. For me Mick's inspiration was jeans and a T-shirt and — brilliant! — a wig of shoulder-length hair which he rolled in a handy garbage can and partially combed.

The house, he said, was in Islington. A derelict street, due to be pulled down, had been taken over by squatters while the Council argued whether to spend money it hadn't got on a tower block which nobody wanted or to make the impossible again habitable. According to Mick, some of the houses could be repaired; some of them, of which ours was one, were too filthy and ruinous. Three squatters had lived there — two youngish men and an amphetamine-swallowing girlfriend of one or both. They belonged to some minor breakaway sect of Trotskyists and had been of use for diverting the attention of the police from Magma. The cell leader, with whom Mick had collaborated during evacuation, had removed them, marking them down for jail fodder when it was needed.

"It's empty, dark and stinks," Mick said. "Keep away from any bedding they have abandoned and watch out for baby shit in the corners! She let it lie."

We have moved in. Mick did not exaggerate except in the matter of the baby shit. It was in a saucepan.

A curious place. The front door has been solidly nailed up. Access is through the basement, where the lock has been smashed. Rotten stairs, decorated with imbecile slogans, lead to two floors above. The curtainless windows of the upper rooms open on to the street so that there we have no privacy, but we are safe from observation as long as we remain in the basement. Any visitor must come down a dozen stone steps before he can get a clear view through the window. There is no electricity, a cracked sink with water and a lavatory with none. I think Sir Frederick can safely stay here while I spend days and nights at large in a pointless search.

Assuming that they now have Clotilde, I see no reason why the committee should delay the explosion any longer. If there is such a reason I must be found and liquidated at all costs, using any of Magma's manpower that is available. They'll know as much as the police. Rex's editor must be in a position to work with Scotland Yard and thus have all relevant inside information.

The reverend baronet has just asked me what I have been writing.

"The confession of Julian Despard," I told him. "If it still exists and is acceptable as evidence, see that your lawyer has it!"

"You have no hope for yourself, Julian?"

"Have you?"

"I shall do my duty as conscience demands. Hope does not concern me or it."

I suppose I can say the same. If the rest die, I die. And if they do not, I somehow don't see myself getting a vote of thanks.

September 11th

Before falling into deep sleep this morning — and dreaming of sea and shore, which always means that inwardly I am at peace with myself — I went over in my memory my last futile attempt at questioning Clotilde. She spat at me the words: "All you know is that it is in a drainpipe." By then she was pretty sure that I had not found out the location of the bomb and that I was trying to provoke her into another slip like that of mentioning William the Builder. So it is highly probable that the bomb is not in a drainpipe at all.

A pipe was useful for packing, for removal to the Hoxton site and from Hoxton to the present site. It could also be a clever device to deceive the police, who were intended to learn of the packing when the murder of Shallope and the investigation of Roke's Tining had proved the bomb's existence. Still another gain occurs to me. Any search for it in drains was bound to cause clashes in the streets, panic in the Cabinet and the maximum inconvenience to a public already loathing the pretensions of its Government.

When William the Builder prepared the cache for the bomb he was not working on drains at all; he was repairing or demolishing something. Failing anything better, I may have a faint clue in Clotilde's assertion that I tortured her to gain information about a secret arms depot. That could be what William thought he was doing.

I have little else. It's now certain that the police and army were never near enough to cause much alarm to the committee. On the other hand, the mention of Argyll Square produced Clotilde's exclamation of William the Builder. A wild guess is that she knew of the cache prepared by this builder some time back and suddenly realized that the bomb was likely to be there. But what has it to do with Argyll Square?

And a hell of a lot of good all that speculation seemed to me when I left my sleeping bag! I never expected to live out the day. Magma had got back Clotilde, which dispelled any reason for further delay. As for the Government, their intentions must be a fog of guesswork. Clotilde was possibly — perhaps already proved to be — one of the women who escaped from Roke's Tining, in which case Julian Despard had her and there was no further point in trying to bargain. Yet there was evidence that Despard and Clotilde were engaged in some sort of violent action and that she was hurt. Are two rival organizations trying to get possession of her? Just a hope — enough hope to wait for a final offer from Magma. They won't get it.

I decided to start my last futile reconnaissance with another look at that house of small flats, 71 Argyll Square. I was very anxious — what a word! I had to force myself to go out — lest my disguise should not be sufficient. In case I was searched by the police I left my knife and Clotilde's .32 at home — a home even more revolting in daylight than at night and no place for clean metal.

Mick had told me not to worry about looking too old for my T-shirt, jeans and long hair, and impressed on me that I was a mature student who could not find work during the long vacation and had drifted down to London. With this always in mind I loafed from betting shop to sleazy café — squalor as mindless as that of a suburban country club — and passed unremarked. Eventually I found a younger and equally footloose companion who offered me a place to sleep if I hadn't got one — squalor at once dissolved by human kindness — and who was inclined to stroll with me to nowhere. Taking advantage of this invaluable reinforcement of disguise, I led him along Gray's Inn Road and into Argyll Square on the excuse of seeing what a mess the fuzz had made. We walked right past number 71 and I glimpsed only the occupants of the basement — a cheerful young couple who had succeeded in growing a few flowers to surround baby's pram and who could be ruled out at sight.

When I parted from my companion, feeling naked without him, I walked at random through several side streets and noticed that the same dark green car passed me twice — a questionable coincidence. The man beside the driver looked through and past me, but he looked. I thought they were police, circling to get a closer view, so I struck across the Pentonville Road, mingled with the drift on the pavement, and entered a pin-table arcade where I played some absurd and lonely game and meanwhile memorized the faces and clothes of five idlers who had entered the place after me.

Having won some sort of jackpot — to pay no attention to what one is doing must be the right method — I left this joint, stopped at a fruiterer's, and bought three bananas which I ate strolling onwards. One of the five players from the arcade was across the road and following me at a distance. The bananas, as I intended, gave him the impression that I was completely at ease, and he was not as good at fading into his background as I should expect a CID man to be. That was not surprising, for the overextended police were bound to be using recruits, special constables and any half-trained personnel they could lay their hands on.

Still, he was sticking to my heels. If he was in communication by walkie-talkie with the green car, it could bring up reinforcements at any moment to stop and question me. It was plain that I was only under suspicion as a possible Julian Despard, not definitely identified.

I considered what orders I myself would give to a partisan on the trail of a suspect. Watch his contacts. At all

179

costs avoid putting him on his guard. Note where he goes
and whether he is confident. When he enters a house,
report immediately. Well, assuming they worked on
those lines, I'd give them something to get their teeth
into. If I entered a house — not a pub, not a shop, but a
place where I could be living — that would arouse real
excitement but no precipitate action. There was a chance
of rounding up not only Despard but some of his gang,
who could be made to talk.

Trapped in the house I might be, but there were many
ways out of a trap: roofs, backyards, bluff. If, however, I
ran, jumped on a bus, or made any sudden move, they'd
be after me with cars, house-to-house searches and cordons. Put in military terms, by entering what might be my
lodgings I forced the enemy to call in his patrols and
concentrate.

Turning away into Camden Town I came across a simple terrace house with a sign in the window of Bed and
Breakfast. The front door was a few inches open, so I
could go straight in without hesitating or ringing the bell.
I walked down a short, shabby passage into the kitchen,
saying that I could not make anybody hear. The landlady
was a bit nervous about that. I put her at ease with my tale
of educating myself and being stranded in London. I also
apologized for my appearance, explaining that I liked to
conform to the dress of my fellow students, which had
the added advantage of being cheap.

She had no room free and said she could give me one
the next day. To waste time I had a look at it and agreed
that it would do very well. That, however, did not take

long. The smell of bacon from the kitchen reminded me
that I had had no breakfast. It seemed an excellent excuse for remaining and exploring the premises so far as I
could, so I told her that I would gladly pay for a good
breakfast then and there if she would allow it.

She did not hesitate, for by this time we were on good
terms. I remained in the front room till after eleven,
pretending to read the paper with which she kindly
supplied me and keeping steady watch through the white
nylon–curtained window while she was upstairs making
beds and cleaning rooms. I saw nothing but normal
movement in the street. My follower did not reappear.

From the lavatory window I had a view of the other
side, which was much as I expected. Backyards stretched
the length of the terrace, separated by a wall from the
backyards of the opposite terrace. Each little house had a
projecting wing containing lavatory, bathroom and
kitchen, so that the ground plan was like two blunt combs
with the teeth facing each other. I saw no easy way of
escape in spite of the momentary cover to be obtained
between the teeth. The police had only to close the ends
of two streets and occupy three or four back windows
overlooking the yards.

Back in the front room I waited and waited for some
sign of activity. At last a car seemed worthy of close attention, for it was traveling a little too slowly. It was a black
Cortina, not the green car, but it had the same two men in
the front seat and now a woman behind. She was half
turned away from my window and for one careless moment leaned forward to speak to the driver. It was Elise,

taken along because she was capable of recognizing me anywhere.

Then it was Magma, not the police, who were after me. My interest in Argyll Square was known since Elise would have spoken of the mission I had ordered. It could well be that number 71 was now under more permanent surveillance and that my pause in front of it had given me away. But even so, the pursuit did not make sense. Clotilde was safe. At any moment Gammel and I were about to share the fate of our fellow citizens. We could do no harm.

Yet it seemed they were not sure of that. I was considered a danger, however remote. In that case London was not going to die for a day or two. I asked myself why, why the delay? Wouldn't the damned thing go off? Did they need a Shallope after all?

More probably it had to do with politics rather than physics. It was for the thinker rather than the active terrorist to guess the committee's program. What a place it was in which to analyze the policy of the New Revolution — a mean front room, grease of bacon congealed on the plate, a pot of marmalade sticky with the fingers of unknown lodgers! But all familiar enough to Russian exiles at the beginning of the century.

Although Rex had let me into the secret as one of the most fanatical and dependable group commanders — dependent as well as dependable — he had told me little or nothing of the Action Committee's strategy. The gist of what he did say I remembered — and have since looked up in this diary:

"Fear, Gil, fear! That alone will bring the chaos. Fear

that can be revived as soon as it is forgotten. At any time we can renew the threat."

He would be right if the Government had ever revealed that the threat is nuclear.

Therefore it could be, I thought, that they were waiting for the Government to come clean and order evacuation. The motive seemed inadequate if one considered London and only London. But Magma after all was international, and Mallant himself was almost certainly on the International Committee. Magma would not be exploiting the bomb to the full if they merely destroyed the capital and disrupted the social organization of one country.

God help me, I had been one of the leading propagandists and yet I had managed to miss the proposed sequence of events! The bomb should come last, not first. Fire the terror before you fire the weapon. Spread the terror over the United Kingdom and across the Channel. Blackmail in Paris and the Ruhr. In Moscow, too, perhaps. Certainly in New York. One can imagine the effect on plain, gullible Americans, who were even prepared to accept that Martians had landed. And then when hysteria is out of control and reaction and disbelief about to begin, show that the threat is real and set the clock for the meeting of that little parcel of U-235 with its mate.

The police were beaten. Magma had only one real danger to face. Me. Yet there in my Camden Town refuge I was not half so afraid of them as I had been of the police. Magma could not easily collect the manpower for this sort of job, especially since the London cells had been dispersed. Why did they do that at all, I wondered. There must have been a day when they did intend to let the bomb precede the terror — perhaps after the inexplicable search of Argyll Square. Me again. The prospect of execution sharpens the mind wonderfully, as my namesake, Dr. Johnson, said.

Forcing the enemy to concentrate had worked better than I expected. If I had been dealing with the police, we should have had one hell of a chase through those backyards with the odds stacked against me. But Magma — well, there were two games they could play. The first was to walk in boldly, deal with me on the spot, and run for it. I did not think they would risk that even if they believed I was off my guard. I was a trained urban guerrilla and presumably armed; if the first burst didn't kill me outright, some of them were coming with me. That meant publicity with incalculable consequences.

The second expedient was to wait, close off the street with the black car at one end and the green at the other, and stop and question me on the pretense of being police. If I didn't stop, they would shoot me down and race off; if I did, was collared, and yelled for help, they would flash a police warrant at any interfering passerby. Holding for questioning — law or no law, excuse or no excuse — must be becoming familiar to the citizens of London together with all the proper and conventional protests from liberal democrats. The police state was being forced to take over. At least we had been successful in that.

At the moment the well-publicized police activity was a serious handicap. If I walked out of the back door and climbed the party wall into the opposite premises, the good woman was going to be alarmed — not to mention the occupants of the houses through which I must go. Mick as wardrobe manager had overdone my stage costume. I was a nasty, long-haired layabout just right to be an anarchist bomber. I could imagine the row of backyards buzzing like a wasp's nest, with any able-bodied men who happened to be about providing the sting.

I went back to the lavatory window. Leaning far out and looking down the rank of yards I could see that my guess was correct. The black Cortina was waiting around the corner at the end of the row, invisible from the front of the house. The green car and its three occupants were out of sight, but it stood to reason that they were around the corner at the other end. It occurred to me that the police could be the kind deliverers of Julian Despard and that I might leave my hostess with a little romance in her life of letting lodgings, even perhaps with her picture in the paper and an enviable five-second appearance on the telly.

I went into the kitchen, paid for my breakfast, and asked her if she would mind helping the police in a vital investigation. I had come to her house, I admitted, on false pretenses. I was an agent of Special Branch, and my real reason had been to watch the street through her front window. She accepted the story without question. My personality had been pleasant, and she recognized that this new line fitted my speech and my account of myself much better than the dubious mature student.

Would she, I asked, call the local police station for me,

give her name and address, and tell them that there were two suspicious cars, one at each end of the street, claiming to be police cars? I could not take action myself, but I was sure everybody would feel safer if a real police car checked their identity.

With great excitement she did what I asked, telling me that she had been thanked for her information and assured that the cars would be checked immediately.

I waited a couple of minutes and left, crossing to the other side of the street and walking slowly down it. Garbage was being collected and I was able to take cover behind the truck, from which I could just see the hood of the black Cortina. Meanwhile I talked to one of the dustmen, asking how I should apply for that rightly highly paid work. I gathered that he didn't think much of me as a possible colleague, and while we were talking a true police car crossed the bottom of the street and started to pull in to the curb. I turned the corner, walked away unhurriedly, and once out of sight ran for the first bus I saw. A pity I could not hear the conversation with the police! Probably my former associates had a plausible excuse for waiting which could, if necessary, be confirmed. That was a point impressed on all cell leaders.

So I traveled gratefully back to our basement and Sir Frederick, buying for him a pork pie, tomatoes and a quart of beer on the way. He was looking pleased with himself and told me he had been out and about. I was horrified and begged him not to take unnecessary risks. He adjusted his filthy scarf, bent his knees a little, and began to hobble around the room. The white bristles on his cheek and chin could have done with a further day's growth, but in the clothes that Mick had provided he really did look a meth-soaked, revolting old man.

"Would you recognize me?"

I admitted that I myself would not, but pointed out that he was badly wanted and dealing with expert detectives.

"Amateur theatricals?" I asked.

"No, the theatricals of this life, Julian. An actor can never be a leader; he has too little self beyond the mirror. But a leader of men must be an actor. I could not have run Roke's Tining without catching the imagination of my colony. Sometimes it was a strain when what they expected of me did not entirely correspond to reality."

I mentioned that when I first observed him in the courtyard he was worried and grumbling to himself.

"Very likely. A release of tension. Shallope was worrying me and I could see no reason why he should be."

I said that I should not have thought his happy, productive Cotswold life could have given him much experience of the old and destitute slinking from one public bar to another.

"If it had not, I should have felt too guilty to be happy. Always you remember the Anarchist and forget the Christian, Julian. No passerby was ever refused a bed. No passerby left Roke's Tining, if I could help it, without new hope. Some returned often and some wrote me letters. Tramps grow mercifully fewer, and those that remain are frequently old and near death. That is how I know. I wish I could have given them my health and strength instead of imitating now their weakness and infirmities."

An amazing companion, and right about leadership! Was there ever a successful general who was not an actor — at least to the extent that he created a commanding and attractive image of himself?

While he dealt with the pork pie and beer like a hungry youth, I asked him where he had been.

"Not your Argyll Square, but wandering not far off. I was making myself known. I have a room in my daughter's house, but she throws me out every morning because she says I smell and at night I go back. Smell, now," he added, starting on the second pint. "A distasteful necessity. Perhaps I can trust our present lodging to provide it. And this suit begins to exhale mementos of its former owner."

"If you aren't careful you'll have some damned official wanting to know your daughter's address."

"I am too vague for that. I just complain as the old do."

I gave him some account of my day, telling him that I now believed Magma had put off the final decision.

"Then we must be careful not to drive them to it," he said.

He had a point there. I wish Magma did not know that I and probably all three of us are in London.

Mick came to see us in the afternoon, bringing food and the evening papers. He expected to find us bored with inaction and was surprised that I was contentedly resting while I watched Gammel carving the outline of a beech, immediately recognizable, from a piece of broken wainscoting. After telling Mick of my narrow escape, I warned him that he too must be badly wanted by Magma.

We agreed that in future both of us were forced to keep clear of Argyll Square, yet we were up against a blank wall unless we could get the names and occupations of the tenants of number 71.

"Would not the police have them?" Sir Frederick asked.

I pointed out that if Mick asked the police — he was the only one who could — he would have far too many questions to answer. Who was he? Why did he want to know? Whatever he replied, they would have him sitting in front of a table for hours while they checked his past and present.

"I am aware of that," Sir Frederick said. "I was implying that if the police had all their names and could get no further, nor could we."

Probably true, though I was not wholly convinced.

"We do have another line," Mick reminded me. "Clotilde's builder. You and I have a chance of tracking him down if we use our heads."

I went over with him again the very little that I knew, only amounting to the fact that Clotilde, when group commander, had done something or been in on something which concerned both Argyll Square and William the Builder. She might have helped to negotiate a secret arms depot which later became the cache for the bomb. When I claimed to know where it was because I had been needed for some duty after the bomb had been moved from Hoxton, she accepted it.

"You never told me that," Mick said.

"It wasn't important. After she had had time to think it over she knew it was a lie."

"Anything else you know about Hoxton?"

I said that one of my cells had been hotting up the strike at the Hoxton Redevelopment site working through International Marxists. When I came under suspicion of showing too much interest in Shallope, my partisans were called off by Clotilde, who was able to do it because the cell leader had taken her orders for so long.

"The bomb was lifted from Roke's Tining to Hoxton?"

"Yes. And the police were allowed to know it."

"Lord help the little International Marxists! All run in, were they?"

"I don't know. The strike was called off. When the papers played up the search of the site for explosives, public opinion was all for lynching the lot of them."

Mick reminded me that he used to be an International Marxist himself.

"I might find an old comrade at Hoxton. It's worth a try. Do you think it's safe, Gil?"

"Nothing is safe. But I doubt if the committee has any more interest in Hoxton."

"If I go now, I'll catch them coming out. See you tomorrow if there's anything to report!"

He said they'd be a thirsty bunch of buggers when they knocked off, so I gave him ample funds for beer. I still have enough to finance our cell of three and our escape, but I don't see a possible life ahead and I don't think there will be three. As the reverend baronet put it, I shall do my duty where conscience leads.

September 12th

It had to be. Under the circumstances conscience apparently approves of murder. We have managed to hide the body from Gammel but I don't know what to do with it. If we are here long, not all the scents of Araby will perfume this little room. Can I put it down — accurately — to a dead rat?

Sir Frederick was mercifully out establishing an identity among the dregs and in his absence I had written up yesterday's entry in the diary when Mick tumbled down the stairs into our basement, panting that they were after him.

"How many?"

"Just one."

"Did he see you come in here?"

"I don't think so. But he'll know it was somewhere this side of the street."

I asked him to tell me quickly what had happened without details.

"A bloke called Jim offered us both a lift. Kevin knew him and said he was OK. He dropped Kevin off in Whitechapel to take the Underground to Kilburn Park and then he started up and damn near hit a lamp post. So he mops his face and asks me if I can drive him home because he's feeling a bit off. I drove him home to Carrington Street, put the car away in his garage, and told him I had an easy bus ride home. 'Well then, you needn't clear off yet,' he said. 'We'll go upstairs and have another for luck.' I was on to something, Gil, and I wanted more . . ."

I interrupted him. His news could wait. The man in the street was an urgent problem.

"Well, Jim pulled down the garage shutter and we went up a couple of steps through a door into the flat. He slumped on to a sofa and said he'd be all right in a minute. Now, I've argued with enough blokes in bars to know when a man's drunk and all the ways it can take him. I just felt there was something wrong. Couldn't say what exactly. So I watched him when he got up to pour us a couple, and I didn't miss that there was a little something in the bottom of my glass when he took it out of the cupboard. 'Do you mind if I have a pee?' I asked, and he showed me where. I tried the front door. Locked on the inside. So I sneaked down into the garage and began to lift the shutter. It was out of plumb and you never heard such a racket. Down he came. Told me to stand still or he'd fire. He did too. But I'd ducked under the jammed shutter and he missed me.

"I ran. So did he. Not more than twenty yards between us. Then we both broke into a walk, for people were about and staring. You can't run in these days without the public taking a hand. I couldn't shake him off. He was too close. And I didn't want to call in the police."

I said that he could have turned into a pub or any shop that was open.

"I did, and then so did he. Once we were face to face — and all the time his hand was in his pocket. He got on my nerves, I tell you! I kept to where there were people and made for you here. No quiet back alleys for me. When I got to the street at the bottom I ran around the corner like hell and slipped down before he could see me."

Mick was not trained to violence. He was an inspired and reliable agitator. Among militant shop stewards he was more decisive and logical than any of them and a red-hot orator if he had to appeal directly to the men, always convincing in putting across what he didn't believe for the sake of what he did. But one could not expect him to know the tricks of an urban guerrilla.

"Silencer on his gun?" I asked.

"Well, it had a thick thing and made a bloody noise in the garage anyway. Christ, he could have killed me in the flat whenever he liked! I don't see why he didn't."

"Because you're wanted for questioning."

"He'll set the lot of them on us if he finds me."

"Has he had time to telephone since he started following you?"

"No. No, he always kept me in sight."

We went out and peered over the edge of the pavement. There was still plenty of movement — squatters sitting in the porches, groups strolling around in twos and threes. The man had not actually entered our street, and remained a shadowy figure at the corner. Things were no longer easy for him. He could not know whether Mick had gone home or taken refuge with a friend, and he did not want to draw attention to himself by asking questions.

I asked Mick if the fellow would know his real name. Mick confirmed that he did.

"And when he was with you in the pub or wherever it was did he leave you to telephone?"

"Yes."

Of course it was then that Jim got his orders. The

193

group commander or whoever was in charge of the hunt would know that the name was Mick's. What orders? First, to find out where he lived in case I was there too. He must have given that up as impossible when Mick refused to be driven home. Second, to kill him rather than lose track of him.

He had run his quarry to earth, but he had to be careful. If Mick's body were found, as it eventually must be, people in the street could identify the probable murderer. And this Kevin with his mates could give evidence that he had driven Mick home.

Would he risk closing in? I thought he might be tempted. He must have been assured that nobody would make any inquiries if Mick simply disappeared. And so the chances were that he would go down after Mick once he knew in which rabbit hole he was, and play the rest by ear. That suited me, for the only place to deal with him was in the privacy of our basement. We could not let him slip off for a moment to reach a telephone.

I told Mick to go into the foul back room that had been half kitchen, half lavatory, and come out only when I called. Then I went up the steps and into the street when the watcher was looking away. I could not carry any weapon under my T-shirt, so I hid my knife and Clotilde's .32 in the dark corner between steps and pavement, ready to hand when I returned.

Movement in the street was thinning as the squatters and their visitors retired to bed. I, too, would appear to be on my way home — a long-haired layabout of no conceivable danger to anyone. I passed the watcher and said good-evening. He was not a foreigner, as I expected, but a nondescript sort of chap with short hair and short beard whom I would have taken for a skilled hand earning good money. There were cells under the direct control of the committee for special assignments, and it seemed more likely that he was a member of one of those rather than a hired killer.

He stopped me, as I intended he should, and asked me if I knew a Geordie named F . . . It is unnecessary for me to give Mick's real name.

"Yes. Lives in a basement down under number six."

"Shares a room, does he?"

"No, all alone. But you won't find him there. He's been away on a job."

He thanked me and I walked on. As soon as he had turned into the squattery I stalked him in the shadow of the porches and saw him walk straight down the steps into our basement. I gave him a minute's grace — dangerous for Mick, but the fellow might be watching to see if he was followed — and then went softly after him, recovering Clotilde's present on the way. I would have preferred the silent knife but doubted if he would let me get near enough to use it.

He heard me opening the door — a noisy proceeding, for it was half rotten — and had time to sit down and look like a casual caller. When he saw who it was and realized that he had been trapped he raised the gun which he was half sitting on. I was a trifle quicker, and the bullet took him at the base of the neck full front. I had hoped to give him a chance to talk. Thank God he didn't let me, for I should have had to execute him in cold blood at the end.

I called to Mick to come out and help me carry the

body into the lavatory in case someone recognized the shot for what it was in spite of the muffling walls below ground level. Before we had time somebody did, knocking on the door to ask if we were all right.

"OK, mate," Mick replied, putting his head around the door. "Bloody cupboard fell in the sink. Christ, what a home sweet home!"

"God Almighty, you must have been fast!" he said to me, staring at the arm and gun stretched out on the floor.

I replied that I was not, that his late friend was inexperienced, and that I'd like to know whether I had really acted for the sake of this worthless city.

"I think you did."

"Well, tell me later! Gammel may be back any minute. We must clean up somehow."

There was no doubt of what to do because there was no other solution. The floorboards were rotten. We levered three of them up, put him inside, and nailed them back again. I left his gun with him. I had no use for a second and it could be awkward evidence. Then we set to work to scrub and mop the whole floor — cleanliness being next to godliness — and shifted my sleeping bag and suitcase to cover the worst of the stain.

While we were on hands and knees, Mick gave me the missing details of his story. Sure enough, he had found among the men leaving the Hoxton site a former friend from the Northeast named Kevin. They went off to the nearest pub where the second pint got Kevin started on the saga of his life and strikes. Like Mick, he had had enough of International Marxists and was left with no creed at all except a determination to raise hell for whatever boss employed him. A bricklayer by trade, it pleased him when working on office blocks to use every trick he knew to weaken a wall and deceive the gaffer. He swore he wouldn't dream of it on a housing estate for honest wage slaves. A practical anarchist with his own standards of revolt.

Mick asked him if he had had any trouble with the police when they were looking for bombs among the drainpipes. No, he hadn't, though he had planted in one of them a primitive device of sugar and chlorate and let it off with a bit of toy fuse. It was a fair giggle, Kevin had said, with all the bastards flat on their faces.

Were there ever any bombs? Kevin replied that he wouldn't know whether there were or not. But it was funny. The pickets had allowed a truck to drive in and drop its load of pipes. Two days later it returned and picked them up again.

"Did the police check up on why the pickets let them through?" Mick asked.

"You bet they did! We said we didn't mind stuff being delivered. It only mucked up the site."

I knew all about that. My own cell had taken real trouble to see that everything was dumped at the most inconvenient site possible.

What about letting the pipes out again, Mick wanted to know. Well, when the truck called back and the driver and his mate said there had been a mistake, they were allowed to load and clear off. Kevin could not remember who gave them leave, if anybody did. There had been a lot of joking and backchat and no particular reason to stop them.

"Did Kevin remember the name on the lorry?"

"Just what you'd expect, Gil. Groads Construction Company. Kevin had never heard of them. Nor had anybody else, including the police. But he thought he recognized the driver, though he'd had bushy whiskers and a moustache before and was clean-shaven now. That was over a year ago."

Kevin told him how a party of building laborers, mostly Irish, had been working late on a school to be opened the next day by the mayor. They weren't finishing it, he said, but just camouflaging what wasn't finished so that His Bloody Worship would not notice. Around midnight they had a few drinks at the expense of the grateful contractors and then a lot more at their own — the police being squared by the contractors not to notice the noise from the pub's back room. When they finally tumbled out on to the pavement, there was this truck to take them home.

They were all pissed and pie-eyed. The Irish had stopped singing and were about to start a fight to keep up the old tradition when the driver said he had lost his way to Kilburn and could anybody tell him? Of course they all looked out or got out but didn't agree on anything except that the driver was going south not north. It was a narrow street of little shops and houses, windows all dark, and just behind them, across the road, was some kind of Bible-punching church set back on a level with the pavement.

They all yelled at him that he had to turn around, so

what does the driver do with all those drunks dancing around the hood but reverse smartly into the church, knocking down a great chunk of the front. They piled in quick and got out of there, laughing their heads off at such a fine way to start the morning. Most of them were Catholic and the rest, who favored the Workers' Socialist Republic, were all for knocking down any church on principle.

Mick had at once seen the trademark of Magma on this episode. Undoubtedly one or more of our partisans had been encouraging the Irish, who somehow were to be saddled with the blame if things went wrong. The reason why the Action Committee wanted to damage a Nonconformist chapel was, he suspected, in order to have the repairing of it. Informants in the building trade might have suggested half a dozen possible schemes before this, the pick of the lot, turned up.

He asked Kevin where the church was. That was his undoing. Kevin, whose voice anyway was far louder than was safe for a serious militant, shouted across to a man standing at the bar:

"Hey, Jim, a pal of mine wants to know where the church was we knocked a hole in! Somewhere in Islington, wasn't it?"

The late Jim came over and Kevin introduced Mick, saying that he had known him for years and could guarantee he wasn't a nark for the fuzz.

Jim replied that he thought it was in Islington but couldn't remember much except that it was a good party. After joining them at their table for enough time to treat them with double whiskies, he went out on the excuse of telephoning his bird to say he would be late.

"And the rest you know," Mick said.

When Sir Frederick came home he immediately spotted the atmosphere of tension. I explained it as excitement, telling him that, thanks to Mick, we were on the track of vital information. He was pleased with what we had done to the floor and assured us that the next day he would have a go himself at the peeling wallpaper and flaking plaster.

"You can't, Fred. Take it all off and the walls would fall down," Mick warned him. "Besides, there's a job for you."

Certainly he was the best man to find that church, though myself I hesitated to suggest it. I have never been happy with his impersonation of an ancient down-and-out; he answers too closely the description of him so far as height and features go. It must be his confidence which carries him through. There's nothing furtive about him, only an air, accepted and exploited, of moral and physical degeneration.

We told him as much as Mick had discovered from Kevin without going into its sequel under the floor. Somewhere, possibly north of the Euston Road, was a sizable Nonconformist chapel, the front of which had been damaged and repaired at least a year ago. And there ought to be some unknown connection with Argyll Square.

"Where was the school which the mayor opened?" I asked Mick.

"Down by the docks. I should have got the actual place from Kevin, but at the time it didn't seem to matter."

"Assuming the driver of the lorry at least started off from the docks in the right direction for Kilburn, Islington is too far north. But we don't know what he did any more than his load of drunks."

"Jim wouldn't have said he thought it was Islington if it was," Mick remarked. "But Kevin knows his London and mightn't be far wrong. Say it was Camden Town or Somers Town or thereabouts — not far off a possible route from the docks to Kilburn and not far from Argyll Square."

Sir Frederick asked how we knew that the building was a Nonconformist chapel, not a church. Well, we didn't; but Kevin had described it as "Bible-punching," which seemed to rule out the Church of England.

"Bible-punching, as you call it, was of great value in its time," Gammel lectured, "though I fear that the over-emotional aspect of religion which once brought hope to the uneducated now does harm by arousing the derision of the half-educated. You, Julian, will have little sympathy for doctrinal differences between High and Low Church, so I will only express my doubts that this instrument of destruction is hidden in a church mission hall or a Baptist or Wesleyan chapel. For one thing, the interiors are singularly bare. However, I will explore the district. It is fortunate that I know only too well the hard-luck stories which appeal to ministers."

September 13th

Sir Frederick returned this evening with a list of possibles: two off Liverpool Road, some Church of England

201

missions, the Salvation Army. Rather than any of these he is attracted — for the oddest reason — to a late Victorian tabernacle off the Caledonian Road in the right sort of street. A truck could reverse into the front merely by mounting the curb, but it seems likely that it would hit one of the solid pillars on each side of the entrance and do little damage. There is no sign of any.

"On the other hand," he said, "we have the clairvoyant."

I had forgotten all about the tame clairvoyant sometimes employed by the police and the suggestion of the chief superintendent at Roke's Tining that the bomb might be dropped from the air.

"It was the police who jumped at that just because the clairvoyant gave them the word 'fly,' " Sir Frederick said. "Outside this tabernacle is one of those puritanical blackboards and upon it in gold lettering: FLY FROM THE WRATH TO COME. Wrath, indeed! Because to our limited understanding the purpose of Creation often appears cruel, must we forget the ever-present, everlasting graciousness?"

He never missed a chance to remind me that I admitted the glory of this universe and our unknown share in it, though I don't know what Jim under the floorboards would have said about it.

"But, dear me, I am preaching to impatient bellies like a missionary on the spit," the reverend baronet went on. "I entered this place, sang out Hallelujah, and sank to my knees. Such hypocrisy may be forgiven, for my prayer was sincere. A sort of caretaker or churchwarden — by his speech an Irishman and somewhat quick-tempered — saw through my overpious pretense, gave me fivepence, and expelled me."

I asked where the churchwarden came from.

"There was a considerable vestry at the back with its own entrance. Originally it may have provided simple accommodation for a missioner to the poor in what were then some of the worst London slums. Now the caretaker uses it as an office for some business of his own. The affairs of the tabernacle can hardly account for so many papers and files."

"Closed cabinets?"

"No, open shelves. I had plenty of time to examine the interior of this place of wrathful worship and I saw no conceivable spot where a large cylinder could be hidden. The heating was Victorian, with boiler and pipes in full view. There was no organ, only a small harmonium. And I think we may exclude the altar."

The visions of clairvoyants probably resemble our dreams in being full of vivid and incongruous details which show what sort of puppy-fun the subconscious is having with its memories. Here and there, if you train yourself to spot it, may be a truth unrealized by the conscious. I didn't believe or disbelieve in the "fly."

"I must also confess that I have taken certain matters into my own hands," Gammel went on.

I glanced at Mick. The presence of Jim could not yet be detectable, but Sir Frederick had a habit of disturbing a clear, or fairly clear, conscience.

"Come clean, Fred!" Mick said.

"I have been talking to the young woman whom you call Elise."

That, as I saw it, was the end. I asked him bitterly if he had told her that he was the wanted Gammel, Rev. and Bart.

"Bless my soul, I had no need to do that! She is an intelligent young woman and suspected me. She came up and said with authority that with my arthritis I should be in the hospital. You warned me, I remember, of charitable busybodies. I could not avoid replying, and when I spoke she recognized me at once."

"Where was this?"

"Near the corner of the Euston Road and Argyll Square. I had rashly assumed that among so many pedestrians I was safe."

So had I. I could not blame him for that.

"And then I persuaded her to cross the road and sit with me on a bench in St. Pancras Station. To me personally she was not ill-disposed. She told me that you were a traitor to your faith — she really did say 'faith' — and had tortured Clotilde. I replied that what she had admired in you was kindliness and consideration in command, but that she did not know you very well. I agreed that you were ruthless and I had little doubt that you would have killed Clotilde if you believed it necessary to save others; but you would not have tortured her.

"At that she became excited and raised her voice, asking why you wouldn't. I answered that you'd tear any mind to pieces, including your own, but not the body of a beautiful woman."

"And what did she say to that?"

"That she hated you."

It was the first hopeful sign and I began to relax.

"I then asked her if she thought a Christian Anarchist such as I would lend himself to the internecine squabbles of terrorists. I fear she was impatient and implied that Christian Anarchism was a contradiction in terms, even going so far as to say that it was a pity the Russians had not invented psychiatric punishment in Tolstoy's day, since a mental hospital was the right place for him and me. She added that I was on the verge of senility and a child could deceive me. A difficult and spirited young woman! I don't wonder that you were both reluctant to tell her too much."

I must admit that I felt Elise's judgment of him was not far wrong. So did Mick.

"Don't you see that Magma's hired assassins will now be at the corner of this street?" he asked angrily.

"No, Mick. No, I think not. But Elise will be."

I reproached him — but more gently — with forcing us to keep her a prisoner.

"That will not be necessary, Julian. I explained to her that I sympathized with her. Whether one considers the lassitude of our own dear people due to frustration or the death of a million Africans from hunger, one rejects with blazing anger the affluent society. But is its destruction worth the death of four or five million in revenge, I asked her, even supposing it would materially assist the survivors?

"She did not know what I meant by my four or five

million. She said that Gil's policy had been to hurry on the New Revolution by creating chaos and exasperation. A few deaths were to be regretted but could not be avoided.

"I noticed that she did not mention Magma. So to show her that senile or not I was fully informed, I did so myself. I could not remember the precise name of the place you mentioned to me, but Exmoor was enough. I asked her what she thought she had helped to land and she replied that the question should be put to you. I said that I had put it and learned that you had landed uranium for the manufacture of a nuclear bomb.

" 'He knew that?' " she cried. The tone of her voice satisfied me that I had not been wrong in taking so much responsibility upon myself.

"I told her that you did not know. It was when you found out that you became what she called a traitor. She asked me why you and Mick had not trusted her. Because, I said, she had seen so much terrible suffering and felt so much anger that you could not be sure she wouldn't consider the death of millions to be justice.

"She answered that very finely: that she was proud to believe all she did and proud to obey, but she was not a robot. It was then that I invited her to follow me at a distance and see where I went. She was, I think, afraid but did not show it."

I remarked that he was perhaps a little impulsive in sizing up characters quite unfamiliar to him.

"It may be so. But have *you* any complaint?"

Elise was alone when Mick went out to fetch her and,

he said, very lonely as well, pulling nervously at her skirt as if it would cover guilt as well as legs.

Down in the basement she stared at me in silence. When she had seen and recognized my face the day before all the other revolting details of my appearance had not, I think, had time to sink in.

"You should have told me. Are you sure it is true? It can't be true," she said.

Sir Frederick intervened, reminding me that the girl was out of her depth.

"Why does he call you Julian?"

"Because it is my name. Only the committee knows it — and now the police."

"The trained . . ."

She swallowed the last word. Killer, it may have been. Her exclamation carried a coldness which showed she had come a long way from her over-romantic view of me. Torturer, too? Did a shade of doubt remain?

I knew that a rumor had been allowed to circulate among the partisans after my escape. It was good for morale — an example of what could be accomplished for a prisoner and how a future for him could be assured. The fictitious — I hope fictitious — persona of Julian Despard was strong meat for Elise. She was like the counterespionage agent who brings in the spy but averts her eyes from the firing squad.

"Trained to become Gil, yes, Elise. Now, what are your orders and from whom do you take them?"

"The same man you ordered me to watch. I told Clotilde everything. They said I was to go back to the room in Argyll Square where Mick put me and I was already known. I was to watch for you and Mick. That's how I came to spot Sir Frederick at the corner. And I have another duty: to report on a man McConnell who lives at number seventy-one in a ground-floor flat."

"What sort of report?"

"His contacts. And to telephone urgently if any of you visit him."

"What are his contacts?"

"Nobody interesting. Two middle-aged men who could be accountants, local managers of large firms or — well, you know the type. And a priest. In the morning McConnell can be seen having breakfast near the window. He's very exact, always punctual to the minute. That's why the tiger man passed then: to make sure that he was well and not worried or in trouble."

Only a little leap of imagination was needed to arrive at last at the importance of Argyll Square and who this McConnell was. I asked Elise to describe the man.

"Thick-set with a large red face and very determined thin mouth. Pale, rather expressionless eyes. Always in a dark suit. I'd say, well, self-important boss of a department of the district council perhaps. But not well enough dressed."

Sir Frederick nodded, at once recognizing the guardian of the Wrath to Come.

Everything fitted, or would have if the tabernacle had been Catholic. In that case the bomb could be masquerading as a cache of explosives for the IRA. But so far as my knowledge went we never used the IRA as a screen — they were easily infiltrated, mixed in their motives, and a magnet for the attraction of police.

I asked Elise if the priest who visited McConnell could be a Catholic.

"He doesn't look it somehow. Too pompous and humorless."

Mick was on to the solution. Had I considered an arms depot of Ulster Protestants? A church originally founded as a mission by some Bible-punching sect and now carrying on for the benefit of stern, middle-class fundamentalists? A fatuous and completely innocent pastor and a churchwarden or elder or caretaker who was a fanatic and considered a secret arms depot to be in the service of his Ulster Jehovah?

"Gil, it's the perfect setup for Magma," he said. "A child could handle it."

I am almost sure he is right, but we are far from the end of the road yet. We must not forget that Elise was ordered to report at once if Mick or I attempted to contact this McConnell. If we do and are detected the committee cannot risk delay. And if I am seen in or around the tabernacle it would be still more dangerous to delay. Yet I must know what is there although Gammel, whose eyes miss little, thinks it impossible to hide anything large.

Let the police do it? Yes, if I could be sure that they would not raid and would go slowly, first establishing identities and never once arousing enough suspicion for the committee to insert the detonators. And it could be a trap. Perhaps there is nothing there but a pound of plastic hidden in a hassock. I don't underrate the ingenuity of Mallant, planning every step months ahead. The hounds fail at Hoxton, fail at Argyll Square, fail at this tabernacle, and each time Magma learns a little more of what they know and what they are likely to do.

September 14th

I am certain where it is and God knows what happens now. I am writing this up in the early afternoon, chiefly to clarify my mind and stop myself from useless fretting.

I decided this morning that it was safe to take a taxi so long as I dressed decently and sat far back. Sir Frederick had a dog collar with him — I thought he would — together with the black dicky parsons wear below it. So I slipped out of the squattery, bewigged and T-shirted and with a parcel containing Herbert Johnson's last remaining suit, and changed in a public lavatory. The parson then ordered a taxi to take him to Highbury and to drive past the tabernacle. On arrival at Highbury and after a reasonable interval he took a second taxi and passed the place again for a second look.

It was only a box of a building, about sixty feet long, belonging to an obscure sect called Seventh-Day Baptists. At a guess some Victorian shopkeeper had been convinced, probably correctly, of the wickedness of his life and left enough money to build the thing and save the souls of Camden Town's heathen poor.

The front was classical with a pediment and two supporting pillars which were not so imposing as they looked. They were half pillars, semi-circular in section, built out from the wall and unlikely to be carrying the weight of the pediment. Gammel had been right on one point. Reverse a truck too fast into the tabernacle and unless you aimed deliberately at the entrance you would hit one of the pillars. But he was wrong when he described the pillars as solid; they seemed to be no more than a decoration, built of brick and plastered to resemble stone like the rest of the exterior. There was no sign of damage. No reason why there should be. William the Builder had only to repair the hollow semicircle of brickwork, plaster over, and repaint the whole front.

In my necessarily swift reconnaissance I could detect no dubious idlers along the street. There was no need, for any of the drab little houses round about could hold a Magma partisan, and a new block of council flats gave an oblique view of the front of the tabernacle. But it could be unguarded. If I myself were establishing a secret arms depot I should be inclined to put my faith in a single, reliable fanatic and allow no one else to suspect its existence.

McConnell, I take it, is using the vestry as an office for some business of his own — he sounds like an auditor — in exchange for a nominal rent and lay service to the pastor. Most of the time he is on the spot, and when he goes out he presumably locks up church and vestry. So I must get in while he is there, immobilize him, and lock all the doors. I shall have little time — assuming that my visit has been observed — and in that time I must not fail. One false step and up we go. Exactly the same arguments that I have against an appeal to the police apply to me.

Is it possible for Mallant and the committee to know that I have discovered the secret? I think not. They are aware that Mick and I are in London, probably with Sir Frederick. They can draw the likely inference from Jim's disappearance that he found out where we are living. But

Jim is of little importance. They have no evidence that I have at last recognized the link between Argyll Square, the load of drunks, the tabernacle, and William the Builder to do the repairs.

Who the devil can William be? He must have a loyal staff and a secure yard where number plates can be changed and names repainted. That sounds like a complete, well-disciplined cell, outwardly respectable and perhaps coming under direct command, with no group commander intervening.

And how could they be sure that William would do the repairs? One of the elders of the church might have a brother or cousin or in-law who was a jobbing builder; nor could William be sure even if he offered the lowest tender. I doubt if such a small job would be put out to tender anyway.

There is only one answer. William was in on the planning right from the beginning. It was he who suggested the plan because he was certain of being employed on the repairs. His firm was known to the pastor and to McConnell and he had only to turn up on the morning after the accident and offer to do the job for nothing as an offering to the church.

He also had McConnell in his pocket. McConnell did not of course know what that cylinder inserted into the hollow pillar contained. He could have been told that it was a new way of packing explosives or a couple of mortars all ready for the time when the Government clamped down on the paramilitary Orangemen and they imitated the IRA by transferring their campaign to England. It's odd that they should believe the poor old Pope endangers their very dubiously immortal souls. The helicopter pilot who swallowed the story that he was landing arms for Ulstermen was probably another of William's discoveries. Whether they feel that a campaign of arson and assassination would be more effective against IRA cadres in England than the legal, fairly effective methods of the police or whether they hope to frighten the English into obeying the demands of so-called loyalists I do not know.

Mick must get me William's name. The telephone directory should help. William's yard is probably in Camden Town, Islington or nearby, and he may be — for the last year or so — an enthusiastic Seventh-Day Baptist. Once I have his name I can try to bluff McConnell into delivering me some arms. There must be a small stock in the cache in order to keep up the deception.

Later

Mick returned after dark. To my cheerful question as to whether he had had any luck he replied:

"Yes. William the Builder is under the floor."

This is deadly. The climax is on us. Only this morning I wrote that Jim's disappearance would convince them that he had found out where we were living and nothing more. But I never dreamed who Jim Ridge was. The killing or kidnapping of Magma's key man, William the Builder, can only mean that I am in possession of every detail and can put my hand — or very nearly — on the bomb itself. No more delay, however desirable politically. Tonight or tomorrow they act.

Mick had entered the first yard within a reasonable

distance of the tabernacle and told the boss that he believed his firm had done the repairs after a car knocked a hole in the front. He was interested, he said, in the plasterwork. No, they hadn't done the job, but they remembered the accident because the police and insurance company had made inquiries at the time at local yards and transport offices, trying to identify the truck which had done the damage.

At the second yard Mick visited he pretended to be a private investigator acting for a northern insurance company. The manager of this yard said they hadn't done the repairs but he knew who had. The chapel lot, whatever they called themselves, always kept business in the hands of chapelgoers. A firm called Foursquare Builders Ltd. in Kilburn had been employed.

Mick went down to Foursquare Builders and approached the place with caution. They did not have much of a yard, but they did have an old disused warehouse where their trucks and stores were under cover and protected from all observation. The gate was locked. There was no sound of any activities and nobody in sight.

The office was in a small square house opening on to the street. He rang the bell, curious to see who answered it if anyone and ready to run should there be voices and the clicking of a typewriter. A charwoman opened the door and seemed glad to have the chance of complaining to someone.

She had let herself in as usual after office hours and started to clean. But there wasn't nobody still there what there always was and nothing in the wastebaskets and no nasty mess in them ashtrays — Mick couldn't resist imitat-

214

ing her — and the whole lot of 'em must 'ave been and gone and taken a day off.

"They must have forgotten to tell you," Mick said.

"That's it," she agreed. "Mr. Jim 'asn't been in for a couple of days. They thought as how 'e 'ad told me, but 'e 'adn't."

"Jim who?"

"The boss. Mr. Jim Ridge. Was it 'im as you wanted to see?"

So there it is. The cell running Foursquare Building has been evacuated. The London cells, which seemed to have been drifting back, will have gone with them.

While I was discussing the position with Mick, Elise came in. She has been ordered to leave Argyll Square and report at once to a rendezvous in Watford. What sort of a rendezvous, I asked her. A wine cellar.

Sir Frederick has also shambled in with the evening papers, drawing himself up to his full height as soon as he is with us in the basement. Then one forgets what he is wearing. He'd even look well as a winged and ageless Saint Michael about to take off. Such a man will be needed if he survives.

All the papers are special editions, publishing Magma's manifesto as they did when Clotilde was supposedly arrested. The Cabinet and editors who are in the know dare not refuse. It's also possible that Rex himself is in a position to publish and obtained Government permission. Then the rest had to follow suit.

I don't think much of the manifesto. Too woolly. But even I could not have explained the substance and objectivity of the New Revolution in three hundred words. For the record, if I am alive and ever want to attack it, here it is:

TO THE PEOPLE

You have approved the courage of your Government in refusing to deliver to us Miss Alexandra Baratov whatever the threat. Gallantly you, the public, have accepted such heroism at your expense. Has it not occurred to you that Parliament is not sitting and you unfortunately are?

But was it heroism? Let us tell you the truth. Alexandra is safely in our hands. At no time was she held by the police. You have been fed lies. You pride yourselves on your democracy but you are fed as many lies as your comrades under the heel of communism. Remember that in the days to come! You will be the first to suffer and must be the first to lead. Remember it when all Europe becomes a police state without mercy or justice. Remember it when after the bloodshed you take power. And then think long and carefully of the future of mankind.

Ask yourselves what are your needs and whether the delusion of wealth can supply them. Ask yourselves what difference there is between the slaves who built the useless Pyramids and the slaves who work in objectless factory lines. Security of employment was common to both. Both were adequately housed and fed. But what of life? What of its quality? All your truest needs are subordinate to the requirements of profitable production.

What has the State to offer you? War, tyranny under the name of democracy and unnecessary law. Law after law frustrates you and each demands a

thousand petty despots to administer it. Why should
you pay them? Why should your labor feed them?
Love and cooperate with each other, everyone in
work where his or her personal happiness is to be
found.

The right-wing papers are not wholly contemptuous;
the left of course are. None of the editorials writes in so
many words of the nuclear weapon, but it can be read
between the lines that they fear something more deadly
than a concentrated campaign of bombing.

They print the Government's reply. It is pitiable. Mere
whistling in the dark. No suggestion of evacuation. We
may have complete trust, we are told, in the ability of the
State to destroy this nest of psychopathic anarchists. The
leaders are known and their activities countered. What
nonsense! Julian Despard and Sir Frederick Gammel are
the only ones known, and if their activities are countered
it won't be by the police.

There is nothing left but to meet the bomb and salute
it, for one of us is about to die. That tabernacle, as I wrote
earlier, is no place for the police even if they are more
expert than I in bomb disposal. But I see no reason why
Mick and his dear Elise should not escape. He is of no use
to me. His courage and loyalty are infinite, but his specialty is not violence.

I told him that it was now hopeless, persuading him
that the bomb would be fired electronically — which I
doubt — as soon as any of us were seen to approach the
tabernacle. We should leave our basement at once, going
separately so as not to draw attention to a party of four.

"And where shall we meet, Gil?" he asked.

I gave him the Roke's Tining cottage as a rendezvous and said good-bye to them both. A pretty child! The cottage is the last place I intend to visit, but I shall be there in spirit.

"That was merciful, Julian," Sir Frederick said when they had gone.

"No. Simple common sense."

"But you have no intention whatever of giving up."

I agreed that I had not, and he insisted on accompanying me. I had to explain to him that whatever happened in the tabernacle might be brisk and bloody.

"I don't want to have to protect you as well as myself. Stay here at the base. I shall need you later."

"Then you should have taken Mick with you."

"Inexperienced. An added responsibility like you. Yes, he might distract attention from me. But what's the good of that when he could be draped over a pew and kicking his last? And I hope that only diplomacy may be needed. In that case McConnell will be less suspicious of one man than two."

"McConnell will have been sent to safety."

"I am quite sure he won't. After all, they do not want him any more."

September 15th

I do not know myself. I am empty of mercy and fear. Nothing is left but a body carrying disjointed thought about with it. Yet who is writing this? There must be an observer who takes a futile interest in the body and some

218

superobserver who watches the observer. Dunne, I remember, demanded an infinite regress of observers. That is intolerable. Somewhere all must end in a unity. But no such unity has yet been found for the atom, and only the guesswork of religions can pretend to find it for us.

McConnell was the obvious point of attack. I had hoped that two minutes in his vestry office — if I had two minutes — would be enough for me to get a line on whatever business he carried on. Sir Frederick's dog collar, though a childish disguise, ought to ensure an interview with him.

I had to give McConnell time to reach his office. The delay appalled me, but to be caught breaking in was worse. Soon after nine this morning I took a taxi to the tabernacle, made the driver pull up at the vestry door in the side street, paid him while I was still in the cab, and made a dash for it. The door was not locked, and I found McConnell inside with two open ledgers on his desk and some files of receipts. The affairs of the chapel were unlikely to require such meticulous auditing. My guess that he could be a free-lance accountant, possibly for other denominations, turned out to be right. I wished him good-morning and said that I had had some trouble in finding his office, which allowed for casual conversation in which to sum him up. I then told him that I had been recommended to him by a Mr. Hunnybun, one of the charity commissioners.

He looked a little surprised at this, as well he might if he had never had anything to do with that particular bunch of apparatchiks, and I went on to say that my dear flock was organizing a flag day for the assistance of Northern Irish Protestants who had suffered from bombing and murder. I wished to be sure that receipts and expenses would be audited in accordance with the law.

"I do not know this Mr. Hunnybun," he said. "I suppose he is a friend of one of my clients."

"Exactly."

"I could certainly look up the regulations and do it for you. What church or churches do you represent?"

I could see that he was considering whether I might turn out to have wider interests than a flag day, so I rushed straight at it.

"Foursquare Builders Limited."

His red, solid face seemed to lose a little of its impassive rotundity and he asked who they were.

"They repaired your pillar."

"Ah, yes. I remember now."

"My collectors for the charity will be calling on you at ten P.M. for advice. That will be after dark."

"This is very sudden. I am afraid I cannot be here at that hour."

I replied that was quite understood and that I was merely giving him advance notice of the time. He could very well remain at 71 Argyll Square.

He did not respond, waiting for more. It occurred to me that, since nobody was ever going to collect arms, he had not been given any instructions on what to do if they did or how they would identify themselves. On the other hand, Mallant or Jim Ridge or a group commander must be known to him and allowed access.

"Didn't the chief warn you when he was here yester-day?" I asked.

A shot in the dark. It was very probable that there had been a final check or last-minute adjustments.

"You must have been sent to the wrong place," he said, attempting a laugh. "You mentioned you had some difficulty in finding it."

His hands were trembling. McConnell, like so many fanatics, was ready to plot and felt all the better for it. To work for his tribe provided him with an added interest, an added self-respect. He would have been very ready to have arms collected while he was safely at home, but the responsibility of actually arranging it was alarming. My references to 71 Argyll Square, Foursquare Builders and the chief's visit appeared to be sufficient authority, but he had no way of telling.

In his mood of uncertainty an air of confidence and command was going to swing him my way. I got up and locked the outside door of the vestry, very foolishly pock-eting the key, saying as I did so that Mr. Ridge had explained the mechanism to me and I would like to test it so that there would be no delay when we called.

He followed me into the body of the tabernacle, where I first tried the main door, which was already locked. The cache of the bomb was obvious, though inconceivable to anyone who did not know it existed. On each side of the entrance and at the right distance from it was a tall, hand-some oak panel inscribed with the Ten Commandments, half on one side, half on the other. So far as I could reckon by eye, the panels inside the church corresponded, with an unimportant overlap, to the half pillars on the outside, but which pillar had been holed by the truck and repaired I could not know. I guessed at the right-hand one, since below it was an open bookcase containing hymnbooks for the congregation. The catch releasing the panel could be concealed behind it, whereas the whitewashed wall under the opposite panel had no visible crack, recess or protruding brick.

So I plunged for the panel on the right, asking McConnell to give me a hand with the bookcase. That at last convinced him of my bona fides — which was a relief and made it unnecessary for me to draw Clotilde's automatic. I could never till then rule out the possibility that he might be the obstinate type, who turns hero at the last minute.

The very simplicity of the work was enough to avert suspicion. The top shelf of the bookcase was flush with the bottom of the panel and pegged loosely into the uprights. One had only to lift it, with its light load of Sunday school leaflets and missionary pamphlets, to reveal a slit with a spring catch in it. Pull out the catch with one finger and the whole panel could be swung back on interior hinges.

I doubt if the reversing truck could have knocked down any of the main wall behind the flimsy façade of the half pillar. The late Jim Ridge must have persuaded the innocent pastor — with McConnell's help — that the brickwork had been weakened; and so after repairing the pillar he took down the necessary section of the inner wall and replaced commandments four to ten over the hollow.

McConnell protested against swinging back the panel.

The windows at the side of the tabernacle were of clear glass in small diamond panes, too high above the ground to allow a passerby to look into the nave, but not too high for him to see the upper part of the panel. I insisted that it must be opened, pointing out that it was hinged on the window side and that nobody could see behind it. If noticed at all, one would assume it was being cleaned or polished.

At last, with panel swung half back, I was face to face with Shallope's creation, lightly clamped to the bare brick of the half pillar. Since it was in a church, it reminded me at once of a large organ pipe with a diameter of rather more than a foot. It was all of dull steel except for a lower section, or breech block, made of brass and about seven inches long. It was this which Shallope had told me I must unscrew.

To deceive McConnell there was a stand of three Armalite rifles on one side and on the other two good old Lee Enfields leaned contemptuously against the wall but in guardroom condition. Underneath the bomb were two small cases of ammunition for both and an open box with five detonators remaining in it. I said casually to McConnell that the new cylindrical packing for explosives was most effective.

"Oh, that's what it is!" he answered. "I wondered."

I examined the base of the bomb with the utmost caution. Running my fingers gently behind it I found a tight wire soldered to the steel and threaded into the brass cap. Try to unscrew the cap and the slightest turn would break the wire. Neat. There appeared to be no way of removing the charge of conventional explosive without detonating it. I wish to God I had known that the only purpose of the wire was to detect any attempted interference.

The wire threw no light on the question of whether the bomb was to be exploded electronically or by clock. Breaking it could bypass either. Rex had spoken of hoping to be far enough away "when the hands of the clock come around," adding that he believed his nuclear physicist found a clock unscientific. But Shallope had not confirmed that. He said he had prepared it all and definitely mentioned a timing device for his explosion in the Western Approaches.

Magma possessed and had developed a number of reliable devices and I thought it unlikely that they would go in for electronics. Without knowing much about the possibilities I could see that the transmitter would have to be powerful, at a safe distance, and operating on a wavelength that nobody else could be using even temporarily. A tall order except for the armed forces and an unnecessary complication. So I was fairly sure it would be timed.

I asked McConnell at what time the chief had called. He replied that it was about half past eleven the previous night. I found that my knees were involuntarily knocking together. It was then twenty past ten. If the chief had set the timing device the explosion could not be later than half past eleven. One does not make the clock circle more than once. At any moment it must go off.

I felt an overwhelming, unthinking temptation to tell McConnell what the long cylinder really was and get him to telephone the police while I myself escaped. But what the hell was the use of that? There was no escape. Whether I stayed or ran the result would be the same.

The tabernacle was silent. McConnell was silent. The tube was menacingly silent. I put my ear to the breech block and could detect no ticking. Higher up against the cold steel I expected, quite illogically, to hear something, perhaps a fizzling as if the thing were getting steam up, although I knew perfectly well that the two masses of U-235 would remain dead as two packets of dust till they were joined in matrimony. Nothing that Shallope had told me helped.

McConnell confirmed that he did not expect the pastor, that he had been in earlier and did not usually return till midday. At least that gave me time without interruption, failing the final interruption. I wanted, I said, to get at the top of the column and needed a stepladder. He fetched one, for he was now nervously obeying. He had read enough in the papers of bombs in drainpipes and was putting two and two together. He must also have heard the rumors passing from mouth to mouth and pub to pub and office to office of an atomic bomb.

Hidden from the windows by the open panel, I went slowly up the ladder, rapping the steel casing and listening. There seemed to be a slight difference of resonance a little less than halfway up which could possibly represent the space between the two charges, the bigger mass above, the smaller mass resting on some kind of bottom plate above the explosive.

McConnell seemed to be a meticulous caretaker when he wasn't balancing accounts. I asked him if he could lay his hands on pliers and a vise. In silence he produced both from a little tool cupboard at the bottom of the church, and then asked me in the sort of awestruck tone with which he might have addressed the devil:

"Who are you?"

"Ask the chief when you next see him."

I set up the vise on the shelf of a pew and began to withdraw the bullets from the Armalite ammunition, pouring out the propellant on to a sheet of newspaper. I was not at all sure what was in the compound besides TNT or whether it would cut steel. I hoped it would if there was enough of it in a necklace in close contact with the column. The job was a long one and I hardly expected to be able to finish it, but as time passed I began to feel more confident that either the clock or the detonator had failed.

When I had about a couple of pounds I packed them in a choirboy's gown, screwing it up tightly and tying it around the cylinder just below the point where the larger mass of uranium should be, and inserted the five leftover detonators with one in the middle and four around it — a target I could not miss with a rifle bullet from halfway down the aisle. The plan was wild, but in view of the delicacy of the construction I hoped that any explosion would disturb it; either the upper mass would fall out or the channel inside the tube would be so distorted that the lower mass, when fired upwards, would shoot out at an angle and fail to combine.

Concentrating on my work of sabotage I was careless, never thinking of any world outside. If the pastor returned unexpectedly he could hammer on the door as long as he liked. True, there could be expendable partisans left behind to keep watch on the tabernacle who might have telephoned the committee that a suspicious character was about. But there was nothing that they, in safety many miles away, could do about it.

I had chosen at leisure one of the Lee Enfields and was loading it when I heard a car stop at the side of the tabernacle and the vestry door being opened. I expected that it would be the priest, who would naturally be able to let himself in, and cursed myself for not leaving the key in the lock. I dashed halfway down the aisle and threw myself flat between two pews. Whatever McConnell said to the intruder — if it was not the priest — I could get a shot at the row of detonators from that position. Two people entered. I heard McConnell go forward to meet them with an exclamation of relief.

I did not dare raise my head to see who they were until I heard a shot and the fall of a body — an event which could be trusted to draw the attention of all concerned away from the pews. The new arrivals were Mallant and Clotilde.

The position of the body showed that Mallant had coolly executed McConnell. For a moment I could not understand why, since McConnell knew all about the cache and had been convinced that it contained only explosives and a few small arms. The panel of commandments was wide open, but there might be a dozen reasons for that. Mallant's only motive for so ruthless a murder must be to eliminate an awkward witness who, if he escaped, could identify the pair of them. If he escaped? But then there was a risk that he might, and we were none of us quite so near to annihilation as I believed.

And what was Clotilde doing with Mallant? One possible explanation was that she had been brought in as an expert, as good a one as Magma had, who already knew of the existence of the bomb but not till now where it was hidden.

In that first moment I could make a guess at what had happened, though some of it may be hindsight. I had always been puzzled by the late setting of the clock. A delay of three or four hours was more than enough to get out of range of the explosion and the firestorm; a delay of eleven was unnecessary folly. Of course the answer was that either the detonator or the timing device had failed. The chief who, according to McConnell, had called at the tabernacle around 11:30 P.M. was Mallant himself. It ought to have been Jim Ridge, perhaps the only other man completely familiar with every detail. Mallant had set the clock, but a brilliant chief of intelligence does not necessarily have the experience of his trained partisans. Dare I surmise that the mind was too brilliant and that after congratulating himself on completing the menial task of meticulously checking and rechecking the wiring he had forgotten to wind the clock?

Clotilde's first act was to cut the wire which I had not risked touching. An effective fake. She gave the brass breech block a half turn to ensure that it was in order. Then she went up the steps to remove the necklace. She knew what it was for, though not, I imagine, what effect it would have on the bomb. I had to decide. I could have waited. I could have let her unscrew the rest of the breech block. But I might be unable to stop her resetting the timing. I might be discovered and killed by Mallant before I could interfere. It was a split-second decision, partly influenced by the fact that Mallant had started to investigate the pews and glance under the altar. When he was turned away from me I raised the rifle and fired.

How long is it since I had any free will? Her head was nothing but a formless mass of red and gold. On to the pink-gray jelly that had been Clotilde poured a continual trickle of harmless, colorless gravel which was U-235. The top of Shallope's monster had been blown clear off.

Jim Ridge's repairs to the outer face of the pillar had also suffered. Through the cloud of dust was a streak of daylight. I had a quick shot from the waist at Mallant and missed him. He replied, but I don't know where his shots went. He was near enough to the blast to be shocked and shaky. Then I was out of the vestry door and in his waiting car, still carrying the rifle, hand automatically stuck to it. I had to get clear and back to the basement quickly. Julian Despard's fingerprints were all over the steel of the tube, lightly at the bottom, very well impressed on what remained of the top.

I tore off eastwards, looking for somewhere to abandon the car. Among the crowd rushing towards the tabernacle when the dust had settled, someone must have noticed the color and number and the clergyman with a rifle in his hand. It was unlikely that I had more than five minutes before a complete description of me was broadcast over the radio in every police car.

It then occurred to me that one of the station car parks was the obvious refuge and, better still, one of the many depots and goods yards behind St. Pancras. After ripping off my clerical collar I turned into the first one I saw.

Nobody paid any attention to me and I had time to think. I was wedded to that rifle. Clotilde's .32 had only two rounds left in the magazine — not enough for the incalculable future of Despard. All the same, I had no lunatic intention of taking the rifle with me down my leg and under my coat until I saw on the back seat a green, hooded cloak which Clotilde must have used to obscure her face while driving through London streets.

So I rolled my awkward friend in her cloak, securing the ends with the parson's dicky ripped in half. A damned odd parcel! But with its neat black bows at each end it looked respectable. A sapling from my garden to plant on Grandpa's grave, perhaps. Nobody showed any curiosity about it when I dived into the Underground.

At Liverpool Street I took the first bus I saw, then got off and walked a little and took another bus, hoping that I had thrown off direct pursuit and could go safely home to the basement. The danger of being recognized as the bomber had wiped out all fear of being spotted by some brilliant constable or passing police car as a possible Julian Despard.

I slipped safely and unobtrusively into the squattery. Several of the idle on doorsteps must have seen me arrive. I could only hope that they had not looked closely enough to identify the long-haired, T-shirted layabout, the visiting parson who had left at breakfasttime and this latest caller arriving with a roll of secondhand carpet as one and the same person.

Sir Frederick was sitting on his bedroll with his back against the wall, outwardly calm and now carving the silhouette of an ash to accompany his beech. The tranquillity of the man was superb. He could live on a desert island with his faith to preserve his spirit and a couple of sharpened oyster shells to add something new to his restricted world.

I told him where the bomb had been and how I had disabled it. I omitted any mention of Mallant and Clotilde, but it was harder to leave out McConnell. By this time Gammel knew my face and expression too well. My curt story of locking the churchwarden in the vestry made him jump to the right conclusion.

"You can tell me if he was injured by the explosion," he said.

"Yes. He is dead."

"Will the police know you are responsible, directly or indirectly?"

I replied that they would at least know I was among those present. In fact they must have had three murders chalked up to my account, not reckoning Jim Ridge.

"And that parcel is the rifle?"

"Yes. I thought I had better not leave it."

He said that he would make it the work of what remained of his life to see that justice was done to me. I let that go. A fat chance he had! I had helped to smuggle in the uranium. I was in on the secret till I could no longer bear it. The judge, anxious to believe the shreds it was possible to believe, might ask me if I never had any respect for human life, to which I could only answer: as much and as little as a soldier.

No, it is more likely that in the future, if I can escape, it will be I who tries to ensure that justice is done to my reverend baronet.

We have decided that on the whole it is better to remain where we are until we have seen the evening papers. Unfortunately we have no radio. Nor do we know where to go.

Later

It is unbelievable. Yet I should have foreseen that the first thought of any democratic government announcing that an atomic bomb had been found and disarmed would be: how many votes are in it for us?

On and on goes the now-it-can-be-told communiqué, modestly emphasizing the agonizing decisions of the Cabinet to give a little here and to resist blackmail there. The skill and patience of our gallant police in their exhaustive inquiries is very properly mentioned, with the revelation that they were in hourly touch with the Prime Minister and Home Secretary. I'll bet they were — with the politicians of course at a safe distance from London. Then we have the customary compliment to the citizens who did not panic in spite of rumors and the meaningless threats of social nihilism. That "meaningless" is shameless impudence, implying that the Government was in command of the situation throughout.

And yet for anyone reading between the lines a month hence — if anyone but politicians ever bothers to look back at what they said a whole month before — it should be obvious that the police had nothing whatever to do with the discovery of the bomb.

The plain facts of the story, so far as the newsmen have

232

been able to master them, are correct. We have the death
of Alexandra Baratov by a premature explosion (why at
the wrong end?) and the murder of Mr. Ivor McConnell
of 71 Argyll Square — according to the pastor of the
tabernacle, a faithful servant of the Lord ever foremost in
the fight against the insidious advances of our misguided
Roman brethren.

The car has been found; it had false number plates.
Julian Despard, alias Herbert Johnson, and Sir Frederick
Gammel are wanted by the police. Inner pages give their
life stories. Sir Frederick's is not so full of gaps as mine
and, he assures me, is a remarkable feat of imagination in
the very short time the writer had to compose it. He is
concerned about the headline MAD BARONET. He has always considered himself healthy in mind and body.

There is no word of Mallant. I wonder what he did.
Well, he had the same five minutes before the arrival of
police that I myself counted on. It might not have been
too difficult to hide between pews and join the first bold
spirits to enter the tabernacle. He will still remain unsuspected even when fingerprints are taken from the car.
His must be somewhere on it as well as mine, but it's a
thousand to one his are not on record. In any case, it will
be taken for granted that I drove the car with Clotilde at
my side.

Sir Frederick looked a question at me when he read of
the death of Clotilde. I had to expand my story to show
that I had not intended it. But was I to allow her to reset
the timing of the bomb? He only remarked:

"God forgive the girl! There was so much splendor in
her."

233

I could have said Amen to that if I were able to forget the fair hair with no head beneath it and remember her as she was.

We have some food, but both of us could do with a stiff drink. We must not show ourselves. I wish I had not let Mick go.

September 16th

This is the last entry. How curious that they should think of Julian Despard as a hardened killer, and yet on his record how right — for I have committed still another murder, to them the coolest and most inexplicable of all. They are trying to talk me into surrender. They even have a psychiatrist to help. I'd love to engage the fool in argument but I haven't the leisure for that. I'm busy. Every time that he and the police interrupt me, trying to discover what makes me tick, I lay down my pencil and put a shot through the top of the door to silence them.

What does make me tick? If I don't know, he can't. So let them go on believing that I am a paranoiac with an itch to shoot policemen. They have such patience. It would be simple to open up with a submachinegun from across the road so that I was pinned to the floor. But they won't. We are still a long way from that police state which Magma and I hoped to create, and yet we were right to foretell the fury of the people when crazed by fear and revenge. Brutes! Have they any other standard of civilization than the lust for more and more possessions and the hope of twopence off?

I should know them. I myself, safely in the

background, have employed a handful of rent-a-crowd agitators to fan a minor grievance into flaming resentment.

But I must get on with my record of the facts. The end came quickly this morning. I suspect that some responsible citizen, forced by misfortune to join himself to our band of street-invading rats, noticed the departure of the dubious clergyman and his uncollared return and went to the police with his report. When he added that, so far as he knew, the only inhabitants of the ruin were a long-haired derelict of uncertain age and an old man, it was worth a reconnaissance in force.

As soon as I saw the cars draw up outside I hurried Sir Frederick to the top of the house together with the arms and this diary, which for him could have been the best protection of all. The basement was impossible to defend, so I allowed the police to come up as far as the landing below us. There I stopped them, warning that I would shoot to kill. Gammel was well aware that I did not mean it and was playing for time. He thought I had a plan. I didn't. There was no hope.

They tried toughness at first.

"Come out, Despard! We've got you."

My answer to that was to smash the light fitting over their heads with Clotilde's automatic. The shot impressed them. They settled down to the siege and began their technique of talking us out. From the window I saw television cameras arrive. The ends of the street became dark with people. A truck drove up and extended into the sky a steel skeleton like a fire ladder but with no ladder. It had a box on top, evidently designed to inconvenience me in some unknown way, so I put a couple of rifle bullets through it.

That was pointless and had its effect on Sir Frederick. He was seeing a side of me which was unfamiliar. What did poor Clotilde call it? Battle-happy. But there was no longer anything to battle for.

He demanded that I should trust the police, sending him out to explain to them all I had done. I replied that they were not likely to pay much attention. On the evidence of the papers, all England appeared to believe that what he and Shallope had made was infinitely more criminal than the supposed quarrels and killings between anarchists which had helped to destroy their handiwork.

He continued to insist, so I could only make surrender easy for him. I threw out a note saying that he wished to give himself up and would come out unarmed and with his hands behind his head. It's beyond imagination to think of him armed. But at times surrender can panic the opponent as much as attack.

"The truth will prevail, Julian," he said boldly.

Like Pilate, I asked what is truth, took his hand between both of mine, and covered his quick exit through the door.

Well, what is it? For perfect justice to be done I should receive the George Cross and a life sentence simultaneously — a little beyond the imagination of our apparatchiks. One would need a Haroun al Rashid for that.

Through the window I watched him appear from the basement between two plainclothes police with the regulation blanket over his head. They put him in the Black Maria, got in themselves, and closed the doors. The police at the bottom of the street — a mere three or four of them holding back the crowd for the sake of safety — cleared a way for the van as casually as if directing traffic. There was no cordon. In fact the departure of Sir Frederick was a perfect example of how a regrettable incident should be quietly tidied up in a civilized country. And then I had to watch that fulfillment of Magma's prophecy, when the people would take justice into their own hands.

There were not more than half a dozen ringleaders. I could spot them from my window as the police on the ground could not.

"Get him! He made it. That's the bloke who made it!"

The crowd surged forward on to the van, upsetting it. The few traffic police were overrun. Then someone — can you pick out in a pack of wolves the one who takes the first bite? — threw a match into the leaking petrol. Prisoner and escort escaped the flames by leaping out at the back, and the crowd closed over them. One of the CID men was hurled out like a ball from a rugger scrum. The police covering the front of my houses abandoned their watch to race to the aid of their colleagues. Some high officer, brave enough to defy the law and the consequences, gave the order to fire over the heads of the mob. That dispersed them and left an empty space in which was a lonely, crumpled, flattened bundle of old clothes. Near Sir Frederick was one man of his escort who could crawl and another who lay still.

The police made some arrests at random, unlikely to be the active rioters. They, more experienced, had managed to tunnel through to the back of the crowd in time. A little beyond the burning van, a well-dressed man was disdainfully walking away along the pavement, his whole appearance expressing disgust for the hysteria of the mob in which he had accidentally been caught up. That prowling gait was familiar to me. When he stopped for a moment to say something to an inspector — no doubt offering his name and address as a witness — I saw his face and beard. He would of course be nearby. It was essential for him to know that both Sir Frederick and I were safely dead or, if we were not, to prepare his plans accordingly.

Mallant did not forget much, but he had forgotten the rifle. I reckoned that in all the excitement the watchers would not yet be back at their posts, so I took the risk of kneeling at the window and resting the Lee Enfield on the sill. The range was about a hundred and fifty yards and the rifle not dead accurate. I hit him in the body with the first shot and had no way of telling if the wound was mortal. The inspector at once leaned over him, but his head was exposed. I tried again and this time there was no doubt.

They will wonder why such a crack shot chose a harmless bystander and left without a mark the uniform above him. That may be clearer when they read this diary — unless I am prejudged to be a homicidal lunatic and Mallant above suspicion. As for Rex, the full resources of the police should be enough to establish his identity. When I was a group commander under him I was content not to know it. Afterwards it did not matter to me who he was.

I have removed the miniature incendiary from the cover of my diary. I started it as an aide-mémoire in an intricate, ever-changing position. I went on as if it were a headquarters war diary, recording events and plans for action which needed to be discussed within a conference of myself. And recently I have seen it as the only witness able to exonerate that revered companion who trusted and comforted me. My evidence in court would be tainted. The evidence of my diary after my own death will ring true.

What a record of futility! The preservation of the future herd led me to Magma; the preservation of the present herd led me to oppose rather than destroy. Can one be called intellect and the other conscience? If so, there is such irreconcilable conflict between them that the only winner can be the Unknown Purpose.

To that I appeal in the only way left to me. The sentence I give myself is death. I am the killer who slit up Vladimir, who would not even give Clotilde time to come down from the ladder. And Jim Ridge down there, waiting to be found? Well, we had no hope if he had lived, so that can be justified. Mallant? Perhaps I might have left him to the dubious condemnation of this diary. But that is hypocrisy. I wanted revenge for Sir Frederick, and by God, I had it!

"Come out, Despard!" they repeat. "We've got you."

You haven't. Either you have got something which has no existence or you are about to release it to a more perfect knowledge of that Paxos evening three and a half months ago.

I told them to wait till I had finished writing. Now I have. I must come out firing or they will not kill me. Never mind, you who reaches for me first! You will be shot through the shoulder with the last round in poor Clotilde's automatic and you'll get a medal for it. All I ask of you, unknown friend, or of you next to him, unknown friend of a friend, is to be angry and to shoot mercifully to kill.